DEAD ON TIME
A DCI CROWTHER MYSTERY

BY

DAVID ROPER

David Roper

Copyright

Also by David Roper

Non-fiction:
An Actor's Life for Me
The Baby Trail

PROLOGUE

There is never a good time to die. Although, if one had to choose, a summer's day in early August might be as good a day as any: the sun warm and strong; flowers in full bloom; trees in full leaf, yet to be tinged by the onset of autumn - what could be better? The problem is that the choice is rarely, if ever, granted.

Sir Harold Moorhouse was lucky, therefore, that he would meet his maker on Thursday, August 8th, 1991; a glorious day and one he would have chosen himself, no doubt, had he known that his 82 years of life were destined to come to an abrupt end. Fortunately, he didn't know, so the question of choice was rendered redundant, and for him life stretched out unendingly, it seemed, as he wandered in from an afternoon of weeding the front garden.

Sir Harold lived in a handsome detached house less than a mile from the M40 in South Oxfordshire. He had bought the house in the spring of 1956 and had lived there happily with his wife, Marjorie, for the final thirty years of his time as founder and Managing Director of Moorhouse Engineering Limited. After his somewhat acrimonious forced retirement, some four years previously, life had unexpectedly turned out to be idyllic, with plenty of time and money to enjoy the new-found freedom: winter cruises in search of the sun; spring and autumn in the garden; glorious summers full of friends and relatives to stay.

Marjorie, or Lady Moorhouse as she preferred to be addressed, first noticed the pain when she was planting runner beans. Typical of her, she ignored it, assuming it would simply go away. In any case, she didn't want to worry Harold unnecessarily. That decision turned out to be unwise, and she was forced to contact BUPA when the pain became unbearable. The prognosis was not good. In her worthy, albeit misguided, desire not to burden Harold with her problem, she had left it too late. Her consultant, erring more on the side of his heart's habitually emotional optimism than his head's realistically clinical pessimism, announced,

"I would say you have a good eighteen months to two years."

In the event, she barely made it to the following Christmas, although the speed of her decline was a blessing in disguise. Sir Harold wept buckets at the funeral on New Year's Eve and was in no mood to celebrate the dawning of his own final year, 1991.

As he stood by the desk in his study on that beautifully warm afternoon of Thursday, August 8th, 1991 and listened to the news that John McCarthy had been released after five years captivity in the Lebanon, he glanced at Marjorie's photo and sighed at the state of the world that she had mercifully left behind a little over seven months before. He switched off the radio and was lost in thoughts of what the pair of them would have been doing on such a day, when he heard someone enter the open front door and walk hurriedly along the hallway.

Sir Harold, turning to greet the visitor who had appeared in the doorway, never knew what hit him. The last thing he saw was something like a long piece of metal coming towards him. He hardly had time to blink before it crashed into his skull, and the carpet, which he and Lady Moorhouse had meticulously chosen not long before she died, suddenly came up to meet him. Two more blows and the job was finished.

The visitor wrapped the weapon in a piece of sacking and zipped it into his canvas holdall. Avoiding treading in Sir Harold's blood, now oozing across the expensive and fortuitously stain-resistant Axminster (£12.50 per square metre), the visitor placed a folder of papers on the desk, switched on the answering machine and ran out along the hallway, smiling.

Ten seconds later, the telephone rang and the answering machine cut in:

'This is Sir Harold Moorhouse speaking. Can't get to the telephone.

'Leave a message. Call you back when I'm available.'

If anybody had been in the house, and nobody was, it might have struck them as ironic that Sir Harold Moorhouse had just predeceased his own last words.

CHAPTER ONE

Thursday, August 8th, 1991: 5.30pm

At the age of fifty-three, and with a mere eighteen months to go before retirement, Detective Chief Inspector Colin Crowther might have been forgiven for thinking that his squash playing days were over. They weren't.

On the one-and-only glass-backed squash court at the Pemborough Leisure Centre, Crowther was putting himself through it yet again. With a supreme effort, born more out of desperation than desire, he sent the ball deep into the back corner and finally clinched the match against his closest civilian friend, Ian Harper.

Their twenty-year friendship had begun purely by chance. After a stint with the Metropolitan Police in London, Detective Constable (as he was then) Colin Norman Crowther, sought what he hoped would be the less stressful environment of South Oxfordshire. His hopes were only partially fulfilled. It was true that, on the whole, the stresses of the job were less, but Crowther's apparent lack of ambition and meagre salary had no chance of satisfying Suzannah, his first wife, whose obsession with social advancement meant that she just couldn't see a ladder without wanting to climb it. In an effort to escape the domestic pressure, Crowther joined the Pemborough Leisure Centre. He insisted to Suzannah that he had to 'keep in trim' for his job, and lied, quite convincingly, about having to spend long hours in the gym, the swimming pool and the sauna. It was in the heat of that unisex sauna that Crowther met Harper and their friendship was forged.

There was no-one else in there that afternoon so, having stumbled upon one another, they had little choice but to make the best of it. After chatting away inconsequentially, as chaps are prone to do, and by putting the world to rights and bemoaning their personal lots etc., Harper just happened to mention that he was an electrician. Crowther damn near bit his hand off. The house in Pemborough, which Suzannah had insisted they bought, needed completely rewiring, and he had had a quote that looked more like a telephone number than an estimate. Harper was sympathetic and promised to pop round the following day and see what he could do. He was as good as his word, turned up on time and more than halved the quote. Crowther immediately gave him the job, along with a generous bonus on top. A mercenary start, perhaps, but friendships have been based on a lot less than that, and theirs blossomed from day one.

It was ironic then that the two men, who got on so well together, were quite different in many other ways. Crowther, at just over six feet, was the taller by a good five inches, and his bulkier frame contrasted with Harper's more wiry look. One mutual friend later described them as being like 'a prop forward and a scrum half'. Also, in contrast to Crowther's rather chequered marital career, Harper's track record in that department had been one of continuity and fidelity. He had been married to Mary for just shy of twenty-six years, and their kids had grown up happy, well-adjusted and able to fly the nest with confidence. Mary knew that Harper had a roving eye, but God help him if any other part of his anatomy was moved to follow. It never did. At that moment, however, roving anywhere, apart from the shower or the bar, was totally out of the question.

"Well played," said Ian, as he shook hands with Crowther.

"Good game," came the breathless reply from Crowther, as he slumped against the side wall. "You had me worried there for a minute."

"Yes, I thought I'd won it as well." said Ian, wiping the sweat from his brow with his wristband.

"No, not about winning. I was worried I was going to have a heart attack."

"Well don't die in here, for God's sake, it'd look bad. Mind you, we have got the court for another five minutes, so you popping it might qualify me for a refund - you never know. Anyway, hurry up and recover because I'm damned if I'm carrying your corpse up all them stairs."

"Very touching," muttered Crowther.

At that moment, his new, innovative and virtually brick-sized telephone, which was wrapped in his towel in a corner of the court, announced an incoming call.

"Oh, good God, they choose their bloody moments, don't they?"

He somehow managed to stagger to his feet and get to the ungainly thing before the caller hung up. He was still breathing heavily as he managed to remember how to answer it.

"Crowther… hello… hello… who's that?... Oh, hi… no, I've just walked up the stairs, what do you think? Right… oh, really?... sure…not long…bye."

"Sounds serious."

"Deadly serious. It was Allyson. She's making a shepherd's pie. I've got to find a tin of peas."

"A detective's work is never done, eh?" Ian laughed, as he gathered his gear together and opened the door to the glass-backed court.

"Have you got one of these things yet?" asked Crowther, holding up his new-fangled portable telephone.

"Certainly have."

"Big buggers, aren't they?"

"True, but at least people can get hold of you, even when you're working. Made a difference in my trade, I can tell you."

"Mine too, I suppose. Here, talking of work, can you do me some electrics?"

"Like what, exactly?" Ian said, guardedly.

"Lights in the garden. She's been after some for ages, and it's her birthday next week."

Ian paused in the corridor by the changing room, and sighed. "Go on, then. Have you got the gear?"

"All but the cable. I can get some tomorrow."

"Don't bother. I've plenty. Sunday morning all right?"

"Cheers, Ian. I'll buy you a drink after."

"That'll be my wages, I suppose."

Ian opened the changing room door and was about to go in.

"All right. Double time on Sundays. I'll buy you two," said Crowther, as he brushed past him and through the door.

Ian shook his head, smiled to himself and padded after Crowther.

"Yorkshiremen! I don't know! You're all just Scotsmen really, aren't you, but without their sense of generosity!"

*

While Crowther and Harper were showering and looking forward to a pint or more in the bar, three miles away Andy Davidson was also thirsting after a drink, as he emerged from the main gate of Her Majesty's Prison, Pemborough.

The prison, completed in 1856 and having four wings emanating from a central point in typical Victorian 'radial' style, housed 562 inmates. Or at least it did until Andy Davidson reduced that number to 561 by walking out to his first taste of freedom in eighteen months. He was wearing the jeans, t-shirt, jacket and trainers he had arrived in, was sporting a smart new haircut and was carrying the rest of his worldly goods in a plastic bag. Thanks to the prison regime he'd lost the best part of a stone and had tightened up all round. As a result he felt fitter than he had for years, and looked it, too.

The Prison Governor and the Probation Service had both been surprisingly helpful, thought Andy, over the question of his future employment prospects and his search for accommodation while on parole. They needn't have bothered. Andy knew exactly what he was going to do and where he was going to do it. He had had everything planned from the moment Her Majesty had generously offered him free board and lodging for three years, with a discount of 50% if he was a good boy. And he had been a very good boy. Not so much to please Her Majesty, satisfying as that would have been, of course, but because of what was waiting for him on the outside. With that in mind, and with a few pints in the nearest pub beckoning him, he set off briskly, his thoughts fixed firmly on the delights that lay ahead.

*

"On your own head be it. And I mean it. Literally."

"Allyson, sweetheart, there is nothing wrong with mushy peas. Best there is."

"In shepherd's pie? I don't think so, Colin."

Crowther's wife, Allyson, had emerged from the kitchen with an oven-proof dish in her oven-gloved hands. Crowther had just finished setting the dining table in his habitually precise way: knives and forks, crockery, wine glasses all gleaming and symmetrically placed. He liked things clean and in order. Allyson placed the dish on a mat in the middle of the table.

"Looks nice, anyway," he said, as he produced a bottle of Liebfraumilch from the sideboard.

"Never judge a shepherd's pie by its crust…"

"…Confucius say."

Crowther uncorked the bottle, as they settled themselves down at the table. Allyson had changed the skirt and blouse she wore for work at the County Bank for the more casual look of open-necked cotton shirt and track suit bottoms and was looking relaxed and comfortable. She tentatively edged a serving spoon into the pie, which emitted a small plume of steam.

"I should let it cool a minute," Allyson paused and watched Crowther start to pour out the wine. "I saw a nice pair of black trousers in Marks the other day."

"Oh, yes?"

"Yes. Size 10. £35. Turn left as you go in, and second display on the right," she said, trying not to make it sound like a set of geographical coordinates. As hints go it was somewhat on the 'heavy' side, it has to be said. However, Crowther was so busy pouring the wine that, although he heard what she said, he totally missed what she meant.

"Did you get them?" he replied instead.

"No, not yet. But it is my birthday next week, so I might."

"Good. Get them if you want them. Why not?"

Crowther had finished pouring the wine.

"Cheers." he said, raising his glass.

Allyson, like most women in such a situation, couldn't work out whether her husband was infinitely adept at secretly taking the point, or infuriatingly inept at blatantly missing it.

"Cheers," she replied, hoping the former, while secretly fearing the latter.

They had not even got to the bit where the glasses 'chink', leave alone brought them to their lips, before the telephone on the sideboard rang out.

Allyson gave Crowther an old-fashioned look and withdrew the spoon from the dish of shepherd's pie.

"I'll keep it warm for you." Resignation crystal clear in her voice.

"Promises, promises," teased Crowther, proving her wrong about his ineptitude at taking the point and, at the same time, adeptly turning her mild reproof into an amusing double entendre. However, all that failed to impress her, so he went for the phone and tried a different approach:

"Anyway, cheer up you old pessimist, it might be a wrong number!" he said, picking up the receiver and turning to face Allyson as he answered the call.

"Crowther…right, and when was this?" he asked. As he listened, he looked at her and shrugged apologetically.

"Where?...Oh, yes, gotcha…yes, I know it…I'm on my way."

He put the phone down, shrugged again and slipped his suit jacket on.

Allyson got up and went to him.

"Will you be lat…" She just stopped herself in time. "Silly question."

"I'll do my best," Crowther said, as she was straightening his tie. He put his arms around her and looked concerned. "Why? Is tonight the night?"

"No…not really. It'll keep. Honestly. Go on, off you go."

Crowther kissed her on the forehead and headed for the door. Allyson sighed in resignation. There was something about never knowing when or, God forbid, *if* he would return that made her miss him even before he had gone.

They had married seven years previously, when he was a 46-year-old divorcee and she was a 27-year-old spinster. At the time, the age gap of a generation had not bothered either of them. Granted, there had been occasions over the years when the difference in their ages had been brought into sharp focus. Like the time they were in the Halifax Building Society, opening an account for Allyson, and the teller had asked…

"Has your daughter had an account with us before, sir?"

…or the moment, during Allyson's thirtieth birthday party, when it suddenly dawned on Crowther that in the same week she was entering this world, he was entering the world of the rookie copper. The age difference came into its sharpest focus, though, when Crowther turned fifty and realised that he was an ever so slightly paunchy, middle-aged man with an ever so pretty, petite wife, who had only recently turned thirty. None of this ever occurred to Allyson, however, although she did sometimes wonder if Crowther was starting to show disturbing signs of turning into the proverbial 'grumpy old man'.

On the whole, though, their relationship had been a good one, unlike Crowther's first marriage to Suzannah, which, if truth be told, had been a divorce-in-waiting from shortly after the Reception. As Crowther had joked incessantly and irritatingly for years afterwards, 'Sad day all round that was. Even the cake was in tiers.'

If it hadn't been for the daughter they produced in year one, that marriage would never have seen its first anniversary. As it was, their daughter, the now twelve-year-old Helen, had held Crowther and Suzannah together as long as they could stand it, which ended up being a very creditable four years. Miraculously, Helen came out of it all relatively unscathed. She also inherited the more positive side of her mother's ambitious nature, along with her father's insight and intelligence, a combination that made her more like twelve, going on twenty.

Allyson was drifting off into thoughts of what a child of theirs would be like, when Crowther slammed the door on his way out and brought her dreams to an end.

*

Sir Harold's house had not seen so much activity since the Moorhouse's Golden Wedding celebrations of 1981. The Garden Party given in their honour had actually been arranged by Lady Marjorie Moorhouse, herself, and was universally recognised as being the highlight of the year. In her opinion, which many of their influential friends shared, it had rivalled any of those at Buckingham Palace. The fact that Her Majesty the Queen had a previous engagement at Balmoral and could not attend Marjorie's 'do', did nothing to dim Lady M's enthusiasm for displaying to all and sundry the letter from the Palace declining the invitation and signed 'Elizabeth R'.

On this day, though, in 1991, a rather different throng had gathered.

Two police cars and two unmarked cars were parked in the drive. At the gateway, a uniformed police officer was keeping a contingent of the Press and a collection of members of the public in ignorance of what was going on, principally because he didn't know what was going on either. Among the crowd was Jack Cunningham, a seasoned reporter from the local newspaper, The Pemborough Herald. No doubt he would be on the phone to his editor as soon as he could prise any information out of the police.   Jack hoped that that would be before the national papers and the regional TV station got wind of events and were hot-footing it to the tiny hamlet of Ardley, home of the late Sir Harold Moorhouse.

Crowther had driven as fast as he reasonably could through the early evening traffic. He turned into the lane, which ran past the house, to be greeted by the sight of a gaggle of people blocking the gateway. He stared at them for a moment, before driving on. He wondered why it was that these crowds always seemed to be made up of the same sort of people. Who were they? Where did they come from?   And how did they know to come here? Perhaps they belonged to some secret society that issued them all with identical clothing and was perpetually tuned in to police radio transmissions ready to order them to rush to a murder scene or a car crash at a moment's notice. Crowther's thoughts were interrupted by the need to get through the small crowd and into the driveway. He sounded his horn, and the Uniform on duty ushered the people to one side, allowing him to slowly ease his car passed them. Jack Cunningham, notebook and pencil ever at the ready, immediately recognised the Detective Chief Inspector and rushed forward to try and get some sort of quote from him. There was nothing Crowther could tell him, anyway, so he waved him away and parked next to one of the unmarked cars.

There were lights on in the house, although it was not long after 7pm and the sun had still not set. Sergeant Trevor Beech, an old school copper if ever there was one, greeted Crowther as he got out of his car.

"Evening, sir. Detective Sergeant Banks is in the house."

"Right, Trevor," replied Crowther, immediately getting down to business, as they walked towards the front door. "What have we got?"

"Sir Harold Moorhouse; big shot engineer; semi-retired…"

"…but totally dead." Crowther threw the remark over his shoulder and entered the house.

"Second on the right, sir. The study."

A scene of crime officer (SOCO), wearing his white overall and shoes, came out of the study, carrying several evidence bags.

"Am I all right to go in, or should I get togged up?" asked Crowther.

"No, you're all right, sir, we're as good as finished."

"Thanks."

DS Banks was standing by the desk, which was largely covered in soil. Sir Harold's body and the carpet next to it had also been the recipients of what looked like a tray of plants, spilled everywhere.

"Sir." Banks was taking off his protective overshoes and turned from the desk on hearing Crowther's voice.

"Evening, Banks. Let's have a look."

Banks stepped aside and revealed the body. Crowther stared at it for a moment, then turned away.

"Good grief. That is horrible! Have you eaten?"

"Not yet."

"Very wise. Neither have I, thank God. What's all this mess?"

"Potted plants, sir."

"What?"

"Potted plants. Geraniums, actually."

"I know what they are, Banks. What are they doing here?"

"A Mrs Rowntree brought them. A neighbour. She found the body. That's when she…"

"…dropped her Geraniums, yes, I get the picture. Can't say I blame her, all things considered. It's a wonder she didn't throw up."

"As a matter of fact she did, sir, just over there by…"

"Yes. Thank you, thank you. Where is she now?"

"At home. DC Liz Collins is calming her down and getting a statement. Given the circumstances, I thought it best to send a female round to deal with her."

"Yes, of course," Crowther murmured, being pretty damn sure that that last remark had as much to do with misogyny as it had to do with sympathy. Banks still had a few gaps to fill in his personal and professional life skills. However, the time wasn't right to go into all that, so Crowther ploughed on regardless. "So, what have we got so far?"

Banks produced his notebook and proceeded to rattle off its contents.

"Sir Harold Moorhouse: early eighties; lived here thirty-odd years; no sign of forced entry or a struggle. Cause of death; several blows to the head..."

"No! I'd never have guessed."

"...with something like an iron bar, no trace as yet, resulting in massive haemorrhaging. Death; virtually instantaneous. Time; somewhere between 4.00pm and 6.00pm today. Those are unconfirmed first impressions, of course."

"Of course. Pathology evening classes fun, are they?"

"Huh! He's long gone, sir. Never seen anybody go over a body so quick. His dinner was getting cold, apparently."

"Typical. Cast-iron stomach has that man. I've always wondered how his wife can stand living with him, you know. I mean, fancy having breakfast every morning with a Pathologist. Whenever he takes the top off a boiled egg, she must wonder if he uses the same technique when he's slicing the top off somebody's hea...oh, stop it, Colin, for God's sake, you'll give yourself nightmares!" Crowther turned to the other SOCO, who was just leaving, "You finished with the phone?"

"Yes, sir," replied the SOCO. "The answering machine was on, by the way, but none of the messages had been replayed, not by us anyway, and we've rewound the tape. Last message timed in at 5.23pm today. They're all listed in there," he added, handing over a list of forensic details.

"Good man. Thanks. OK if I press this?" asked Crowther, pointing to the message replay button.

"Like I said, we've finished. Press whatever you want. Be my guest," said the SOCO, making his way along the hallway.

Banks couldn't wait to show he was on the ball, and piped up as the SOCO was leaving,

"I've already listened. I can tell you what's in the messages."

"I'd like to hear them for myself, if you don't mind."

"Sir."

Crowther pressed the button and listened to the playback.

'Harold. It's Edith. I'll pop round in a while with those plants, if that's all right. If not, ring me. Bye.'

"I guess that must've been Mrs. Rowntree - as in geraniums," explained Banks.

"Yes, I suppose it must've been. Thank you, Banks," replied Crowther.

The answering machine 'beeped' its way to the next message.

'Hi, it's John. Sorry about the noise. We're on the train, just leaving Oxford.' (A loud whistle and what sounded like a train moving off could be heard in the background) *'I'll try you in half an hour. Cheers.'*

Crowther, in expectation of some informative comment or other, looked at Banks, who simply held up his hand as the machine 'beeped' to another message.

'It's John again. Nearly at Banbury now. You're obviously still busy, so I'll call you when we get back home. Cheers.'

Banks turned off the machine and proudly announced, "That's it. And that was John - as in 'who the hell's John?' No idea. What we do know, as the SOCO said, is that that second call from John, the last call, was received at 5.23pm today. So, if he made that call half an hour after his first call, as he said he would, then he must have made his first call somewhere before 5.00pm, and in any event shortly after Mrs. Rowntree, who made the first call on the machine. Speculation, of course, and dependent on him doing what he said he would, which he may or may not have done, obviously."

"Yes, obviously…I think. Well, thank you for making all that crystal clear, Banks. More to the point, at the moment, is; why was the answering machine on at all?" Crowther wondered aloud.

"The front door was propped open, and it seems as though he'd been working in the garden, so that's probably…" Banks suggested.

"Yes. Makes sense. And he was killed in here?"

"Looks like it, sir."

"So maybe he came in to listen to any messages."

"But never made it."

"That much certainly is obvious. In that case, the killer was either already here, or followed him in and struck before Sir Harold had time to hit the replay button. It's an estimate, of course, but time of death ties in with that as well. I wonder," Crowther mulled over the possibilities as he wandered out into the hall. "What about the neighbours?"

"We're doing house to house in the village, and one of the local Uniforms has gone to find the paper boy. Says he knows where he lives."

Banks indicated an unopened newspaper, with what appeared to be a bloody footprint on it, lying in the hallway.

"Is that the killer's print, do we think?" asked Crowther.

"Unfortunately, it's not, sir. It's Mrs. Rowntree's. We don't know if the paper boy saw anything, or exactly when he delivered the paper, but she says it was on the mat when she arrived and she slipped on it as she ran out."

"Poor woman. She must have been horrified," said Crowther, as he looked around the hall and glanced into the adjoining rooms. "Nice house, isn't it? Wonder what it's worth. Bet you wouldn't get much change out of a million for this little pile. Look at that lounge, very classy. My wife would love a place like this, you know. So would I, come to that; except for the gardening, of course. Still, you can't have everything. Although, I don't see why not…every other bugger seems to have it."

Crowther had always wanted to live in a house in the country. He was born and brought up in Yorkshire, amidst all the woollen mills and associated industries of the West Riding. His only escape had been to the Dales, where his mother's sister, Aunt Kate, ran a B&B not far from Grassington. He would go and stay with her during the school holidays, and he loved it. So much space and so few people; so much quiet and so little noise. He often wondered what life would have been like for him now, had he opted for the country life and a B&B of his own. But the lure of a career in the Police Service had led him into a much more metropolitan existence, and he had to admit that he didn't entirely regret being drawn in that direction, even if it did mean moving 'down south' in the first instance.

By the time Crowther reached the front door, lost on his fantasy journey into the world of 'what might have been', Sergeant Beech had arrived to bring him back to reality.

"Sir. The local bobby's just called in. Apparently, the paper boy saw two people, he *thinks* they were men, leaving the house on foot just after five. He said he was in too much of a hurry finishing off his paper round to take much notice of them or where they went. He also said that the front door was open, and he left the paper on the mat. He didn't see Sir Harold."

"Where's the boy now?" Crowther asked.

"At home, sir. Shall we bring him in?"

"No, leave him. He's better off at home. Going down the station might freak him out. Have a quiet word, Banks, and see if you can get a bit more out of him than that local copper managed. The boy must have noticed something about them. Were they wearing coats, hats, gloves? Were they carrying anything? Did they seem in a hurry? Was there a car nearby? You know the sort of thing. It's amazing what people have got stored away in their brains and don't realise it. Go gently, though, eh? He's only a lad. Oh, and make sure DC Collins gets all the gossip she can out of Mrs. Rowntree. I have a feeling that 'our Edith' might be the fount of all knowledge round here."

"Right, sir," Banks said and headed for his car through the assembled crowd.

"I'll see you both back at the station later, after I've sorted out this load of storytellers," muttered Crowther, as he braced himself for the customary onslaught of unanswerable questions. He often wondered why the Gentlemen of the Press bothered to turn up at this stage of the game. They all knew damn well that they would get either a non-committal answer or a statement of the bleeding obvious, so why bother?

"Good evening, gentlemen," he announced, politely, as he faced a phalanx of The Press, whose numbers had miraculously grown while he had been inside inspecting what remained of Sir Harold Moorhouse's head. From the way they were jostling one another for position, it was painfully obvious that they were all desperate to pounce on some sort

of quote, no matter what, if only to justify their existence. Undoubtedly, and true to form, the majority would opt for a sexed-up version of 'a statement of the bleeding obvious', ending up making 'less-than-nothing' sound like the scoop of the century. .... *'Detective Chief Inspector Colin Crowther, senior investigating officer (SIO), did not deny that the police had not questioned anyone in connection with the discovery of a body, nor that it may or may not be that of Sir Harold Moorhouse, the alleged owner of the house.'*....and treating us to a meaningless feast of double and possibly triple negatives into the bargain. A classic case of:

'The irreverent in hot pursuit of the irrelevant', thought Crowther, at a 'Wilde' guess.

*

Meanwhile, in one of the upmarket leafy avenues of suburban Pemborough, Andy Davidson asked the taxi driver to drop him on the opposite side of Castle Avenue from where he wanted to be. He needn't have taken a taxi at all from the pub where he had celebrated his release, but the mere fact that he could was an irresistible temptation. To have money in his pocket, however little, and the freedom to do with it as he wished, was a feeling that only a recently released prisoner could possibly experience and appreciate.

Andy was supposed to go to a *halfway house* on the other side of Pemborough, which the authorities had provided as his accommodation until he acclimatised himself to life on the outside and found a job and his own place to live. He had every intention of going there and fulfilling the terms of his parole, for the simple reason that he had absolutely no intention of stepping out of line and being sent back to prison to serve the rest of his sentence. It was no Holiday Camp on the inside, whatever anybody said.

However, Oakridge Lodge, the house that he was now staring at longingly, was where he knew he was going to end up. It was a large detached house, one of many in the tree-lined avenue, and was set in more than an acre of land. Of the five bedrooms, two had walk-in wardrobes-cum-dressing rooms and all had en-suite bathrooms. The master bedroom overlooked the beautifully kept garden at the back and had an excellent view over the adjacent Pemborough Castle Golf Course and of the bunkers surrounding the ninth green. On the ground floor, an elegantly furnished through-lounge led to a large, and equally elegantly furnished, conservatory, which in turn had French windows opening out onto the swimming pool and pool house. Andy had only been inside the house a couple of times, but he felt he knew it well, and had often visualised what life would be like there, as he day-dreamed in his prison cell. Those dreams were about to become reality, and he could hardly wait. There was only one thing he wanted to see more than the house and that was its occupant, preferably naked. She filled his thoughts yet again.

At that precise moment, just as his fantasy was hotting up, and him with it, a blue BMW 600-series turned the corner to his right and cruised towards him. Andy, half-hidden by one of the large oak trees along the avenue, recognised the car and was eagerly awaiting his moment to surprise the driver, once she had brought the car to a halt in the driveway. He was about to cross the road when he realised that she was not a 'she' at all, but was, in fact, a rather fit-looking young man, who got out of the car, locked it and went to the front door. Andy assumed, quite reasonably, that the car was being delivered back after a service or something and that the young man would ring the door-bell. He didn't. Instead, he opened the front door with his own key and strode in as if he owned the place.

The smile that had been creeping across Andy's face in anticipation of surprising the woman disappeared in an instant to be replaced by a look of utter bewilderment. Questions bombarded him from all sides: Who was the young man? What was he doing driving *her* car? Why did he enter the house in such a proprietorial fashion? All the answers seemed to lead to the same disturbing conclusion. Andy stared at the front door in disbelief, trying to decide how the hell he was going to deal with this apparently disastrous twist in his situation.   Finally, he crossed the road.

*

Crowther had never been a coffee man, preferring the good old English cuppa above all else, even when dispensed by the vending machine in the corridor along from his office. The trouble was that whenever he tried to use the machine it seemed to take offence and refuse to co-operate.

He had returned from Sir Harold's house, made notes on what would be needed to pursue the inquiry and was dying for a 'white, two sugars'. He inserted the appropriate coins, pressed Tea and was waiting patiently, when DS Banks and DC Collins arrived.

"Oh, for God's sake!" Crowther exclaimed. He banged the side of the vending machine and heard his coins drop, but without the slightest trace of any activity from inside the machine. "All I asked for was a cup of tea, for crying out loud."

"Big mistake. If you wanted Tea, you should have pressed Hot Chocolate," offered DC Collins.

"Silly me. Of course I should. Obvious when you think about it. Have you got any change, by the way? It's just swallowed all mine."

Collins rummaged in her shoulder bag and came up with a purse.

"Here we are, sir," she said, handing him several coins.

"Thanks. So, what's new?" asked Crowther, ramming the coins unceremoniously into the slot.

"Collins!" Banks barked out what sounded more like an order than an invitation to speak. She hated him treating her like some sort of servant, about as much as he loved lording it over her, and he was at it again.

Banks was thirty-three, just under six feet tall, fit and ambitious. He was good-looking in that kind of slightly swarthy, heavy-eyed and, if you like your ice cream runny, Italian way. He had neatly trimmed dark hair, was always very smartly dressed and reckoned on making it to Chief Inspector long before the age Crowther had been when he got his promotion.

Banks's big problem, though, was DC Liz Collins. He had never quite understood the bond there seemed to be between her and DCI Crowther and he had long harboured the fear that she might be promoted over him. It was not an entirely irrational fear. Collins had often exhibited those two qualities most essential in making a really good detective: intuition and luck. Banks had good qualities too and was, without doubt, efficient and thorough, but it had pissed him off on more than one occasion when his subordinate had scythed through the jungle of facts in a case and hit on the one thing he had missed. However, on this occasion he felt that he had an ace to play, would bide his time and definitely keep it up his sleeve.

"After you, Collins," he deferred, with a condescending look to Crowther, who ignored it, since his attention was fixed firmly on the vending machine.

"Thank you…sir," she replied between clenched teeth. "Mrs. Rowntree, Edith to her friends…don't press Tea!" she almost screamed it out.

"What! Oh, my God, don't do that! Scared me to death." Crowther only just managed to stop himself pressing Tea and hit Hot Chocolate. "Hot Chocolate. Yes, of course. Thanks, Collins. You were saying?"

"Yes, sir." she continued, referring to her notebook to get the details correct. "Edith Rowntree says that Sir Harold founded Moorhouse Engineering Limited not long after the Second World War, during which he had been involved in developing the high-speed Mosquito fighter/bomber for the de Havilland company. It was made of wood, she told me, although I think she'd been drinking, quite frankly."

"Maybe she had, but she was right. Hard to believe, I know, but Mosquitos were made of wood and were one of the best, but it's a long story," said Crowther, suppressing a laugh.

"Oh, I see. Sorry. Anyway, Harold (they're on first name terms, by the way) had been living in the house in Ardley since the 17th October, 1959…"

Crowther looked questioningly at her.

"…that was the day before her birthday, apparently, hence her being so specific. Rumour has it, and she would know, that his retirement four years ago was not entirely voluntary, although, uncharacteristically, she didn't know the details. She told me that Harold now works as a part-time consultant to the company, with special responsibility for high specification engines. However, ever since his 'mysterious retirement' (her words), he is no longer involved in the day-to-day management of the business, but still holds his shares. His wife, Marjorie, who considered herself to be 'a cut above', but who was 'no better than she should be', according to Edith, died of cancer last year, just before Christmas. Sir Harold has one daughter, Anna, married to a John Goodland. They live in Brighton."

"That would be the John on the answering machine, I suppose," said Crowther while watching the machine filling a plastic cup.

"Possibly…"

"Probably, sir. I agree." Banks couldn't stop himself muscling in.

"Possibly the John on the answering machine, yes." Collins couldn't stop herself emphasising the uncertainty of Banks's rather sycophantic contribution. "Brighton Police are going to visit. Sir Harold had no particular friends in the village, apart from Edith, of course, and no enemies either, apparently. Hardly ever went out since his wife's death. He would just potter about in the garden and do the odd bit for his company, or rather ex-company."

"Doesn't tell us much, does it?" said Banks, dismissively.

"Tragic, though, isn't it? But then again, if he was happy, why not? There are many people a lot worse off in this world," mused Crowther, gingerly picking up the plastic cup and setting off along the corridor towards his office. He turned to Banks. "So, what about it, Banks? How did you get on with the paper boy?"

"Pretty well, sir. Now, this really does tell us something." he announced, his glance to Collins not going unnoticed by her, as he intended. "The boy himself couldn't add much, so I thought I'd have a word with his father. Good job I did, because it turns out that he'd seen the two men earlier on. The good news is, we know who they are…"

Crowther and Collins turned to him, expectantly.

"…the not-so-good news is…they're Jehovah's Witnesses."

"Are they really? Well, they're my witnesses now." Crowther was taking a sip of his drink. "Bring 'em both in. If Jehovah has a problem with that, refer him to me…" he held up the cup. "…and this is coffee!"

*

Andy Davidson didn't know that the temperature in early August 1991 was going to be pretty high and neither did he care. All he did know was that it was a pleasantly warm evening, but all he cared about was who was doing what to whom, and why, inside the house that he considered to be his rightful home. The sun was slowly sinking behind the golf course clubhouse, bringing dusk to Castle Avenue and in particular to Andy and the occupants of Oakridge Lodge.

After he had watched the young mystery man close the front door, Andy had walked casually, or as casually as he could, given the circumstances, across the road, around the side of the house and along by the wall that marked the rear of the property. When he reached the spot where he reckoned he would get the best view of the swimming pool and patio, he climbed onto the low branch of an old oak tree and stood on it so he could see over the wall. Having successfully, if depressingly, put two and two together, what he saw didn't entirely surprise him, but it still came as somewhat of a shock. Stretched out on a sun lounger was the object of his lustful prison dreams, Janice Holloway, wearing damn near next to nothing. Through the open French doors, Andy could clearly see the young man, now stripped off down to a pair of skin-tight swimming trunks, pouring himself an iced drink and carrying it out onto the patio.

"Want a drink, Janice?" he said.

"Later. Come here," she replied, as she slid off the lounger and stood provocatively before him.

The young stud walked over to her, took a swig of his drink and kissed her on the forehead. Much to Andy's increasing anger and bitter disappointment, Janice responded by wrapping herself around her new lover and kissing him full on the mouth. They stood locked together. He fondled Janice's right buttock with his left hand, while running his ice-filled glass down her back with his right. Janice giggled, gently disentangled herself from him and dived into the pool. She surfaced after swimming a full length underwater and breathlessly called, "Jason, turn the lights on will you, darling, and come on in. I might have something for you down here!"

Jason dutifully flicked a switch by the patio door, smiled knowingly at Janice and executed a rather impressive dive, as the pool and garden lights came on. The whole effect was of a quite idyllic scene: stunning sunset; subtle lighting of the trees; Janice and Jason illuminated in their coupling. To a passer-by, the stuff of dreams; to Andy Davidson, the stuff of bloody nightmares. By now he was absolutely furious and was about to leap over the wall and swing for the pair of them, when a thought occurred to him. He looked at his watch, mouthed *shit* and dropped to the ground. The conditions of his parole had caught up with him, and he had to get to the other side of town in under twenty minutes or face the consequences.

Andy had just started jogging along the road at the far side of the house, when he saw it. It was attached to one of the corner pillars of the wall, for all to see.

"You bitch," he screamed to the world in general. Whatever anger was simmering inside him had come to the boil in that one moment: the moment when he saw the sign saying:

FOR SALE

CHAPTER TWO

Friday, August 9th, 1991: 9.30am

Outside the Pemborough branch of Tesco's, in Cathedral Square, the daily open market was up and running. Stallholders and customers alike were getting into the swing of another trading day. The supermarket was part of The Cathedral Centre, Pemborough's new shopping mall at the southern side of Cathedral Square. Open barely 3 months, Tesco's had already started to affect the turnover of the market traders in the square and the small shops surrounding it. Pemborough Cathedral, from which The Centre, as it was commonly known, had stolen its name, looked down as reproachfully as usual.

None of all that, it has to be said, was foremost in the mind of Detective Constable Liz Collins on that Friday morning, as she walked past Tesco's and out of The Cathedral Centre, on her way to Pemborough

Police Station in Priory Street. True, she had never gone a bundle on The Centre, or on any shopping mall come to that, but whatever corporate vandalism the Council and the Developers had visited upon poor old Pemborough, Cathedral Square, with its market stalls and traders made up for everything in her eyes. Little did she know how short-lived her pleasure in those quaint and ancient rituals of commercial life would be. For the moment, though, all she knew was that she adored walking through Cathedral Square, especially at this time of day, when it was in full flow. Because of the rising heat of the day, she had taken off the jacket of her pin-striped suit and slung it over her shoulder. Even so, she could feel her white shirt beginning to cling to her back, as she strode past the eclectic collection of market stalls.

Pemborough had woken that Friday morning to the news of yet more mysterious 'crop circles' appearing across the country, and, closer to home, the more immediate and often personally distressing news of Sir Harold Moorhouse's murder. Several people were studying rather skimpy newspaper reports of both stories, and groups of locals could be seen gossiping in the shade offered by the market stalls. DC Collins passed the local branch of W.H. Smith, outside of which was a Pemborough Herald newspaper hoarding:

MOORHOUSE MURDER
POLICE BAFFLED
IS KILLER IN OUR MIDST?
'CROP CIRCLES' – LATEST

She resisted the temptation to buy a copy, on the grounds that the fanciful speculations of the Press always made her either laugh or despair. As she turned the corner of Cathedral Square into Priory Street, she spotted DS Banks coming down the steps of the police station.

"You don't really expect me to believe you've been in there all night," she said with mock seriousness.

"Someone has to do the work, Collins. Back in a minute. I'm going for a paper."

"Get me a sticky bun, will you?"

"You mean: Get me a sticky bun, *sir*! But watch it, you'll get fat."

"OK. Make it a diet sticky bun, then…sir! Is the DCI in?"

"Not yet," Banks replied and set off towards Cathedral Square.

Liz Collins watched him go and wondered what on earth she had found attractive about him during those first few weeks. Whatever it had been, it had long since disappeared to be replaced by a general irritation at his superior attitude, mitigated only by the occasional bout of good-natured banter such as they had just had. She turned and took the steps up to the main entrance two at a time.

*

Allyson Crowther was sitting on the bed with a thermometer sticking out of her mouth. By her side was a printed piece of paper marked out as a graph. At the top it said:

OVULATION: TEMPERATURE CHART.

Down the side were 'degrees' (97, 98, 99 etc.) and along the bottom were 'days' (Day 1, Day 2 etc.). The idea was that by recording the daily temperature throughout a menstrual cycle and noting significant changes, it would be possible to get a good idea as to when ovulation was taking place (i.e. when eggs were released from the ovaries). Then, or around then, would be the ideal time for fertilisation to be possible and, therefore, for intercourse to take place. It was one of the very first steps on the road to conception for the one in six of couples who, at any one time, were experiencing unexplained infertility.

The Crowthers, for instance, had been trying for a baby for nearly a year, and their impatience, particularly Allyson's, had got to the stage where it had started to get them down. For one thing, she was coming up to thirty-five, her 'conceive by' date, that dreaded age beyond which the odds against conception become progressively longer and the time left to 'get it together' becomes distressingly shorter.

When they were first married, children had been way down the agenda. Crowther's divorce settlement had left him pretty potless, and maintenance payments for Helen accounted for most of what he had left at the end of the month. Allyson had to work to pay the mortgage and keep a roof over their heads, and it was only with the help of her parents that they had managed to hang on to the car. However, Crowther's somewhat belated promotion to Detective Chief Inspector, five years ago, had eased the burden considerably. So much so that during the last couple of years they had not only accumulated a modest level of savings, but had also paid off the Building Society, enabling them at last to sleep the sleep of the un-mortgaged.

No doubt, it was this new-found feeling of security that had contributed to Allyson's hormones beginning to stir deep within her. She had always thought she would get pregnant one of these days, but when it dawned on her that 'these days' were rapidly becoming 'those days', she realised that she desperately wanted a baby.

At first, Crowther had been enthusiastic in his contribution, both emotionally and physically, but as time went on, and he edged ever nearer to retirement, doubts had started to creep in. He had seen the future, quite selfishly, as revolving principally around him, with his home, his wife and his daughter by his first marriage providing comfort in his retirement. He felt that he had done his bit, made his contribution to society and deserved a well-earned rest. Having said that, he had every intention of being the best father he could, should he ever be called upon to fulfil that role. It was just that if it wasn't to be, then it wasn't to be, and, if he were honest, a significant part of him would breathe a hefty sigh of relief.

"I'm off," yelled Crowther from the foot of the stairs. "Allyson, I'm off! Do you want dropping at the Bank?"

"No, it's all right. See you later," she mumbled through a mouthful of thermometer.

Crowther made his way up the stairs and into the bedroom.

"What did you say? he asked. "Oh, sorry. Didn't realise you were in the middle of that."

Allyson took the thermometer out of her mouth and squinted at it.

"I said: I'll see you later. I've got the morning off. Good Lord! Either this thermometer's dead, or I am.

"Let me have a look," said Crowther, grabbing it off her. "You're right, you know. You must be dead. Hardly moved, has it." He took out his lighter and applied a flame to the base of the thermometer. The mercury shot up like a rocket and cracked the glass top. "It's moved now. Sorry. I'll buy you another one."

"Thank you, Nurse."

"My pleasure. Funnily enough, I was wondering what to get you for your birthday. Problem solved. See you later."

Crowther hurriedly made his escape.

Allyson picked up the chart and sighed.

*

Banks was strolling back towards Priory Street, reading a newspaper and carrying Collins's sticky bun, when he saw Crowther scanning the window display in Knickerbox. Without looking up from his paper, he passed Crowther and, stifling a grin, said, "Morning, sir."

"Morning. Oh, yes, right. Morning... erm... David," muttered a slightly embarrassed and flustered Crowther. "Just window shopping..."

"Worry not. Your secret's safe with me."

"...for my wife's birthday," he emphasised, with a smile.

"Of course, sir."

"Presumably there's no news, since nobody called me."

"Nothing. Dead as a doornail..."

"Why can you never find a Jehovah's Witness when you want one?"

"...and the Goodlands aren't back until Monday morning."

"The daughter and son-in-law?"

"Yes, sir, and we don't know where they are."

"Blimey. It is going well, isn't it?"

"It certainly is." muttered Banks, who was distracted by reading his newspaper, wasn't really listening and missed out on Crowther's ironic comment. "Here, get this! According to the paper we '...have not ruled out anything in our enquiries.' How true."

"Yes, although personally I'm not banking on suicide."

"And listen to this: apparently, we are '…still puzzled as to the motive for this brutal murder.' Oh, come on, give us a chance! 'DCI Colin Crowther, who is leading the investigation, said last night…'"

"Let's have a look." said Crowther, grabbing the paper and starting to read. "Oh, so that's what I said, was it? Course it was. Here, talking of motive, have we got one yet?"

"Well, as far as we know nothing was taken and, on the evidence, whoever did it only went into the Study, so that seems to rule out thieving. As for anything personal, Sir Harold seems to have been a well-liked bloke and kept himself to himself. In other words, no. No motive."

"Terrific. What about his company. What was it called?"

"Moorhouse Engineering Limited. Actually, I'm going round there later on this morning to see the Managing Director, a Mr Graham Kirk. From the correspondence we found at the house, Sir Harold seems to have been working on some gearing system, presumably for them, but that doesn't tell us much."

"Don't knock it. For all we know, it might be a highly competitive, cut-throat business."

Crowther was still studying the paper. "Good grief! They do write some bollocks, don't they?" He looked up from the paper as they were passing Boots, the Chemist. "I'm just popping in here. See you later."

Banks held out his hand expectantly, but his newspaper had already disappeared into Boots, leaving him standing outside, looking somewhat miffed. Banks turned and headed for Priory Street, still clutching Collins's sticky bun.

*

Outside the front entrance of Moorhouse Engineering Limited's headquarters, Graham Kirk eased his shiny black Range Rover into the space reserved and marked for him as Managing Director. Because of the heat of the day he emerged from his air-conditioned cocoon in short sleeves but was wearing black 'Genuine Lambskin Leather' driving gloves; just one of his many affectations. He put on his jacket, which had been hanging by the off-side rear window, and retrieved his 'Airline Pilot' briefcase, another affectation, from the back seat. After ostentatiously locking the vehicle with its remote, he pocketed his personalised key ring, took a last look at his pride and joy and entered the building.

Melanie Hebblcthwaite, seated at the front desk, was answering a call in that sing-song way that seems obligatory for receptionists the world over.

"Moorhouse Engineering. How may I help you…hold the line, please. Mr. Kirk. Mr. Kirk…"

"My office," barked Kirk, as he swept through reception, ignored the lift and bounded up the stairs.

Melanie muttered, "Pig," and went back into sing-song mode for the benefit of her latest victim. "Sorry to keep you waiting. Moorhouse Engineering. How may I help you?"

Kirk had disappeared round the corner of the stairwell, so he missed the intriguing sight of Miss Hebblethwaite speaking while sticking her tongue out at the same time, a trick she had developed specifically for her dealings with Kirk, or 'God Almighty Graham' as he was affectionately known by the girls in the office.

Three floors above Melanie, Miss Stannard, Kirk's secretary, looked up from her word processor as Kirk swept into the outer office. In her fifties and dressed from head to toe in Marks & Sparks' best, she had an air of authority about her and was the only person in the company who seemed to have Kirk under control. In fact, rumour had it that Miss Stannard knew enough about him to put him inside for the duration, but that was only wishful thinking. She peered at him over her glasses, looked pointedly at the clock on the wall, and said, "Afternoon, Mr. Kirk."

"Yes, yes! I know, I know," he replied gruffly and marched into his private office. Normally, he took timekeeping extremely seriously and was rarely, if ever, late for anything. That particular morning, however, delays to his normally clockwork routine had been caused by a sleepless night, brought on by the events of the previous day, and which had left him with a lot to think about. Added to that, a delegation from the Engineering Union was due at lunchtime for a meeting, which had all the makings of being rather tricky. Consequently, his arrival so late in the morning was doing nothing for his state of mind, leave alone for his reputation for punctuality and, inevitably, for his stash of Brownie Points, with which he bolstered his standing in the eyes of the redoubtable Miss Stannard. After slinging his briefcase onto the leather settee by the window, Kirk took off his gloves and slumped at his desk.

He had been followed into his office by Tom Marchbanks, Moorhouse Engineering's Financial Director. Tom was one of those people who looked constantly worried, probably because he was.

However, he had no real reason to be; he just took his work terribly seriously and was never quite satisfied with the way he did it. On top of that, he felt personally responsible for the ups and, particularly, the downs of the company's finances. Sir Harold Moorhouse, in his days as Managing Director, had relied on Tom to keep him up to date with the company's financial health, and had valued his well-thought-out advice above all others. When Sir Harold retired, Tom simply carried on as normal under the new incumbent, Graham Kirk, and continued to speak his mind where matters of money were concerned. That frankness, which Sir Harold had cherished, was simply an irritant to Kirk, who just wanted Tom to get on with his job and leave him in peace to get on with his.

That kind of division of labour might well be acceptable in many circumstances, but in the case of a Managing Director's relationship with his Financial Director it was simply not on. Kirk's narrowness of mind meant that he was incapable of grasping the importance of the bigger picture. Tom had tried to get him to step back, as it were, and take a broader view of the business, but Kirk would have none of it. He was an engineer, pure and simple, and that was that.

On that particular morning, all Tom Marchbanks wanted was to bring certain facts to Kirk's attention in the hope that he might show at least a glimmer of interest in the running of a successful business.

"Graham, I've been looking for you all morning," said Tom. "Is everything all right?"

"Not now." Kirk picked up the phone on the desk.

"Only I've got those figures to show you. I thought we…"

"I said: not now!" exclaimed Kirk, through gritted teeth. He turned his back on Tom and pressed a button on his phone console.

"Get me Peter Feldman asap," he demanded and slammed the phone down.

"It'll only take a couple of minutes, Graham. Look, it's to do with…"

Tom opened the file he was carrying and went round the desk to Kirk's side with a sheet of paper.

"I've got too much on. Go away!"

"It really can't wait. We need to come to a decision today."

"Get back to your abacus, Tom, and leave me alone, for Christ's sake. I'm an engineer, not a bloody accounts clerk."

"As you wish," Tom replied, suppressing his anger and frustration. "I would simply point out that Sir Harold never once ignored the…"

"Sir Harold is dead, my dear Tom, in case you hadn't noticed. He has left us for good. Why don't you follow his example and shuffle off, eh? There's a good lad," said Kirk, condescendingly.

Tom Marchbanks summoned up as much of a disgusted look as he was capable of, which didn't amount to anything much in the end, and walked out of Kirk's office with as much dignity as he could manage. It was all for nothing, since Kirk, as usual, wasn't taking the slightest bit of notice of him.

Left alone, though, the brusqueness and bullying that typified Kirk's outward persona seemed to leave him and revealed the look of a deeply flawed and worried man. His mind was elsewhere when the phone on his desk rang. It took him quite a few seconds to bring himself back to reality and remember that he had placed a call to his solicitor, Peter Feldman. He grabbed the phone.

"Peter, listen…oh…yes, Miss Stannard, what is it?...who?...right…yes, yes, of course, show him in."

Kirk was thrown into a bit of a panic by not being able to talk to his solicitor, Peter Feldman, but even more panicked by the identity of his visitor. He quickly tidied his desk, took out his pen and started to make notes in his diary. He looked every inch the calm, yet busy, executive engrossed in his work, when Miss Stannard opened the door and announced, "Detective Sergeant Banks, Mr. Kirk."

"Thank you," said Banks, as he entered.

"Please, please come in. Thank you, Miss Stannard, that will be all."

She gave him a cursory nod, knowing full well it was all part of his act, quietly closed the door and returned to her desk.

Kirk had looked up in apparent surprise, for all the world as if he had been disturbed while drafting the Magna Carta and rose to greet his visitor.

"Good morning, Sergeant," he said, all smiles and charm, as he came round his desk to shake hands with Banks. "To what do we owe the pleasure? Please, have a seat."

"Thank you," replied Banks and settled himself in the upright leather chair across from Kirk, who had returned to his 'Director's' chair in front of the picture window. "Just a few questions, if you don't mind, Mr. Kirk."

"Not at all. Would you like a drink? Coffee, I mean. You're on duty, of course." Kirk smiled at his own cliché of a remark.

"Of course. No, thank you. I'm fine." Banks smiled in return.

"Good. So, how can I help you?"

"First of all, on behalf of us all at Pemborough Police HQ, may I offer our condolences on your loss? It must have been somewhat of a shock, to put it mildly, learning of Sir Harold's death, particularly in view of the circumstances."

"So it was. A fine man. Sad business," replied Kirk, gently shaking his head in disbelief, although not entirely convincingly to anyone sensitive to genuine expressions of grief.

'Yes. Yes, indeed it is a sad business, as you say. You knew him well and saw him quite regularly, I expect," said Banks, bringing the conversation back to the facts of the case.

"I knew him, of course, but didn't see much of him of late. Last time must have been a couple of weeks ago."

"So, you didn't see him yesterday?"

"Yesterday?"

"Yesterday. Thursday. The day he was murdered."

"No, no, I didn't see him. No. Definitely not."

Kirk's initial charm seemed to have deserted him, to be replaced by a certain edginess.

"I see.   Just for the record; where were you yesterday?"

Kirk paused and swallowed hard before replying. "I was…well, I was at The Old Ship Hotel in Brighton overnight on Wednesday, and then I drove   back   here   to   the   office…on Thursday…yesterday."

"Brighton, eh? Very nice. So, you arrived back in Pemborough at what time, would you say?"

"What time?   Well…can't rightly remember, although I'm pretty sure I was in this office before six."

"Thank you.   Is there anybody who bore Sir Harold a grudge, do you think? Might have wished him harm?"

"Harold? Absolutely not. You didn't know him, of course, but he…"

The phone ringing interrupted Kirk. He looked at it, then at Banks, smiled rather weakly, picked up the receiver and took the call, "Yes?...ah, Peter…yes, I did.   Look, I've got someone with me at the moment. How about I call you later, eh?...Good man. Speak to you then."

Kirk put the phone down, gave Banks an apologetic look and made a note in his diary.

"Sorry about that. You were saying?"

"I wasn't saying anything. You were going to tell me about Sir Harold. What he was like and why nobody wished him harm."

"Was I? Yes, of course. Sorry. It's been quite a twenty-four hours around here."

"I understand," said Banks, settling back in his chair and waiting.

"Well, there's not a lot to tell really. Harold was well-known and respected by the whole engineering industry. His work during the War on the Mosquito had made sure of that. Personally, he came across as a rather diffident kind of character. He never threw his weight about and was always willing to listen to anybody's ideas, which made him particularly well-liked among the graduates we take on here. As with most highly intelligent people, he didn't suffer fools gladly, but he did have the knack of letting them down ever so gently, without them even realising what had happened, if you understand me."

"Of course. Interesting. I guess yours must be a highly competitive business, Mr Kirk."

"Competitive? Not particularly. The niche we fill in the precision engineering industry is pretty much ours and ours alone."

"A monopoly, you might say?"

"Hardly. Competition exists, of course, but we have it under control."

"Internally? Is competition there 'under control'?"

"Of course."

"No problems here that Sir Harold might have been privy to?"

"None at all, as far as I know. We're a very close-knit, integrated team," replied Kirk, firmly.

"Anything in particular that Sir Harold was working on currently?"

"Not that I know of. As I said, I rarely see him."

"He wasn't working on some kind of gearing or transmission system?"

"For us? Doubtful, that's not really our field. The only work of that kind he might have been involved in would have been for John."

"John?"

"Yes, John Goodland, his son-in-law."

"Right. Why for him?"

"For the car. John's trying to develop a Formula 1 racing car. Harold's always had a soft spot for motor racing, so he's helping him, or rather he was. All goes back to Harold's involvement with high performance engines during the War."

"I see," said Banks,

"Yes. Got his sights firmly set on racing in F1 has John. Could make it, too. Bloody good driver. I've seen him in action."

"One of your interests, too, is it?"

"What?"

"Driving. Formula 1. You a speed merchant?"

"No, no. Not me," replied Kirk, with a sly look at his watch.

"Just wondered. Nice fast-looking car you've got parked out front. It would certainly beat mine from a standing start. You wouldn't happen to know where he's gone for the weekend, would you?"

"Who?"

"John. John Goodland. Any idea where he is and when he'll be back?"

"I'm afraid not. Hardly ever see him.' said Kirk having another quick look at his watch. "Look, I really need to get on. If there's nothing else, I…"

"Of course. I understand. No, that's all for now. Thank you, you've been very helpful."

Banks shook Kirk's hand. "If we need anything more, Mr Kirk, I'll be in touch."

"By all means. Goodbye, Sergeant."

Kirk watched Banks until the door closed behind him, then let out a long sigh and slumped into his chair, deep in thought.

*

It is said that a woman in search of a husband would find a man of average good looks disproportionately more attractive were he to wear a uniform. If true, that may be to do with the excitement and/or romance attached to whatever job the uniform represents (soldier, sailor, fireman, policeman etc.), along with the degree of fitness and authority implicit in that job, or it may be to do with the smartness or ruggedness of the uniform itself. A combination of all those things is a likely explanation, but in the end it would probably all depend on the woman's proclivities.

In the case of Chief Superintendent Anthony Vance, his male proclivities had little to do with the reaction of the opposite sex to his uniform, nor with the reaction of his own sex, come to that, but more to do with his own personal reaction. He just loved being inside his uniform, especially when it was fresh from the dry cleaners. Over and above even that, he was principally interested in being seen inside it by the world in general and by the Press, in particular. His attraction to, and obsession with, his uniform would have fascinated any passing psychologist, and his sense of self-esteem, when in his full regalia, would have sent any self-respecting psychiatrist scurrying to the nearest reference books on 'Megalomania and the Uniform'.

All that apart, Vance was the consummate diplomat. He would have shone in the corridors of Whitehall and could undoubtedly have run rings round any 'Sir Humphrey' who dared to cross swords or, more probably, words with him. However, he had opted instead for a career in the Police Force, on the grounds that his particular diplomatic, political and organisational skills were infinitely better suited to a more rigid and permanent structure than he would ever have found at Westminster. The shifting allegiances, the almost daily changes in policy and the seemingly endless juggling as 'a servant of two masters' would have driven Vance mad. In any case, he also relished the public exposure of Police Press Conferences, exposure which would have been denied him as an anonymous Whitehall Mandarin. In short, he was one of those fortunate human beings who had found a niche in life from which he had no desire to move and in which he felt blissfully contented.

Crowther had always harboured a sneaking admiration for the way Vance always seemed so comfortable with himself and with life in general, although it did irritate him beyond measure that he could never quite put his finger on the secret. How

Vance could react so calmly in the face of both triumph and disaster always made Crowther feel both envious and furious in equal measure. Thus, it was with this habitually ambiguous approach to his superior officer that Crowther found himself presenting a rather meagre resume of the Moorhouse case, late on the evening of what was turning out to be an extremely warm and pleasant Friday.

"I'm afraid, at the moment, that's all we have, sir, and all we can release to the Press. I wish it were more."

"Absolutely. However, you know what these Press and TV chaps are like: instant arrest or nothing. Damn nuisance. Talking of which, better get to the dry cleaners before they close."

"To save you the bother, would you like me to handle the Press Conference, sir?" offered Crowther, knowing full well that such a suggestion was tantamount to sacrilege for Vance, but also knowing that it would somehow be expertly dismissed with a straight face and a quote directly out of 'The Vance Book of Unfazed Answers'. It duly came.

"How very thoughtful of you, Crowther, but it is my job after all and I'm sure I'll cope."

"I don't doubt it, sir. Experience will out."

"Absolutely," said Vance, as he leaned forward, conspiratorially, "secret of handling the Press, Colin, is simple:

You never answer the question they've asked.

You never answer the question they think they've asked.

You answer the question they would have asked, if they'd thought about it in the first place."

"Yes, sir. I'll remember that - when my time comes."

"Absolutely. You in this weekend?"

"Yes and no, sir. Weekend off, allegedly. But I'm on call, obviously."

"Obviously. Nothing doing here then?"

"Very quiet. I'm just waiting to see if there's anything more from Forensics, and the sooner we find these Jehovah's Witnesses the better. They're our only lead so far."

"Absolutely. It's a ridiculous thought, I know, but there's no chance they could have been involved, is there?"

"No such thing as a ridiculous thought in this business, sir. However, getting rid of Sir Harold, assuming he exited in the right direction, if you get my drift, would be a pretty heavy-handed way of keeping Jehovah's statistics favourable, don't you think?"

"Absolutely."

Having thus used his favourite word 'absolutely' five times in less than two minutes, Vance decided enough was enough, and demonstrated his superbly diplomatic way of ending a conversation and dismissing a subordinate.

"Well, thank you, Colin, and let's hope something does arise to disturb your weekend, if you get my drift," Vance smiled, acknowledging Crowther's phrase, and opened his diary.

"Absolutely, sir," said Crowther, pointedly returning the compliment.

*

In the kitchen of their house in suburban Pemborough, Allyson looked up from preparing dinner, as Crowther opened the front door and shouted out, "Allyson! You in?"

"Kitchen, where else?"

He hung his suit jacket on the coatrack in the hall and walked along to the kitchen.

"Brilliant," he said, kissing Allyson on the cheek. "A weekend off. At least I'll believe it when I see it."

"So will I," she replied and turned to look at him. "Oh, what's the matter? Are you going to be all right playing squash tomorrow?"

"Yes, why?"

"Your shoulder. You've not been in a fight, have you?"

"I'm a DCI, sweetheart. They call me in when it's all over…as a rule."

"So what's the matter with it?"

Allyson went to touch his left shoulder, which was hunched up as if injured in some way.

"Nothing," protested Crowther, backing away. "I've just been testing this for you."

He produced a thermometer from under his armpit, examined it and announced, "Ninety-eight point four! It works. I'm alive."

"You're not telling me you've driven all the way home with that thing stuck up your armpit!"

"Not all the way, no. Just the last couple of miles. Mind you, changing gear was a bit iffy, I can tell you."

"Why didn't you put it under your tongue, you daft bugger?"

"Language! Anyway, I did, but I nearly bit the end off when I had to brake hard. And, before you ask, yes, I got some really funny looks at the traffic lights when I tried to stick it up my bum!"

"You're disgusting!" cried out Allyson, trying her best not to laugh.

CHAPTER THREE

Saturday, August 10th, 1991: 10.00am

As the distant Cathedral bell struck ten o'clock and shoppers were scouring the Saturday market for bargains, Andy Davidson found himself yet again hiding behind a large tree in Castle Avenue, watching the front door of Oakridge Lodge.

He still wasn't sure how to handle the situation with which he had been presented on his release from prison two days previously, and it was gnawing away at him. However, when Janice appeared in her expensive track suit, along with designer sports bag and matching boyfriend, Andy glanced up at the 'FOR SALE' notice outside the house and the seed of an idea was planted.

Jason, Janice's addition to the household, kissed her passionately, put the sports bag in the boot of the BMW and opened the door for her. She slid into the driving seat, gunned the engine into life and shot out into Castle Avenue. Jason waved her off and strode back into the house.

Andy had witnessed the touching little scene from his vantage point and watched the BMW's progress until Janice swung it left into Castle Drive and disappeared at speed. He set off after her on foot. He was in no hurry. He knew exactly where she was going and he had plenty of time to get there, which would give him ample opportunity to fill out and finalise the plan that was gradually taking shape in his mind. He was quite pleased with it so far, he thought to himself, which was more than Janice would be!

*

"Colin! Ian's here!"

"What?"

"Ian's here!" yelled Allyson from the kitchen.

"What does he want?"

Crowther was somewhere in the depths of the garage, where he was hard at work shifting stuff around, and his somewhat muffled voice was just about audible from the doorway into the kitchen. Allyson had opened the door and was peering into the gloom of the garage.

"He wants to play squash by the look of…what are you doing?"

Crowther started to quickly manhandle a large parcel away from Allyson's eye-line.

"Oh, yes, squash, right. I'm just tidying up, that's all. You keep out."

"What? What are you doing with tha...?" she stopped talking in mid-sentence and stood in the doorway, open-mouthed. "Awww, Colin, you haven't!"

"Haven't what?"

"You can't have!"

"Can't have what?"

"Bought me a lawn mower for my birthday!"

"You really know how to spoil a surprise, don't you? Funnily enough, that's not a bad idea: you could do with a new one."

"Watch it!"

"Just keep out of here. Off you trot, nosey parker. Excuse me."

Crowther shooed Allyson out of the garage, closed the door and hurried through the kitchen into the hall, where Ian Harper was waiting patiently.

*

The Pemborough Leisure Centre was at its busiest most weekends, and that particular Saturday morning was no exception. The local fitness fanatics had all-but filled the car park, obviously intent on

their weekly dose of exercise. Among them was
Janice Holloway, who had finished her aerobics class
and was about to emerge from the air-conditioned
foyer into the glaring heat of the midday sun. She
was accompanied by Glynis, the sister of her lover
Jason, and with whom she habitually shared exercise
and gossip, in equal measure. They were chatting
away merrily as they came out and headed for the car
park, when a fit-looking young man in shorts and
carrying a sports bag over his shoulder passed them
on his way in. The girls eyed him up and down,
giggling   at   their   view
of his rear end, 'air-kissed' each other and parted to
their respective cars. Janice was unaware that her
progress was being monitored carefully by Andy
Davidson, who was lurking in the shade of the trees
that lined the far side of the car park.

   Crowther and Ian Harper were also at the far side
of the car park, where Ian had just parked his
'Harper's Electrical Services' van in what seemed like
the only available space. Carrying their sports bags,
they passed a jaunty-looking Janice, as they crossed
the car park and made their way to the entrance to the
Centre. Crowther had his phone to his ear.

   "…in   that   case,   get   down   to   Kingdom
Hall…Kingdom   Hall…it's   where   Jehovah's

Witnesses worship, or whatever they do…so go round there tomorrow, Sunday, they're bound to be there then…well, if it's your day off, Parker, ask DC Collins to go…yes, tell her I said so and you have a lie in, son, why don't you!...bye," Crowther ended the conversation, turned off his phone and put it in his sports bag. "Good grief. Where do they get them from? I hope he's on sale or return!"

"Can't get the staff these days, eh?" said Harper.

"It's not so much that, Ian. It's having to wipe their backsides that gets up my nose…I wish I hadn't said that."

"So do I!"

Laughing, they left the car park and entered the Centre.

On the far side of the car park, Andy emerged from under the trees, as Janice was about to open the boot of her BMW. He crept up behind her and gently placed his hands over her eyes. Janice squealed in surprise and dropped her sports bag.

"Oh, my God!" she said, before recovering herself. "I bet I know who that is. Cheeky!"

"I bet you bloody well don't, Mrs Holloway!" Andy whispered in her ear and pulled her head back, gripping her tight.

"Andy?" said Janice, stiffening at the sound of his voice. "No, it can't…"

"Who did you think it was, bitch?"

Andy loosened his grip, turned her round and trapped her against the boot.

"Surprised, are we, Cheeky?"

"Hello, love," said a nervous sounding Janice.

"Don't give me that."

"What do you mean? I just didn't expect to see you so soon."

"Really! Is that a fact?"

"Yes. I mean…how did you get out? I…I thought you'd got three months to go yet."

"I bet you did, but you know what 'thought' did, don't you? You see, I've been a good boy, so they've let me out early to come and play. So here I am. Spoiled your plans, have I, my darling Janice?"

"What plans? What are you talking about? Look, let's go and have a…"

"Drop it, Jan. Do I look like a total idiot? I might have been stupid enough to get mixed up with you in the first place, but I've learnt a lot since then. Took me for a right fool, didn't you?"

"I don't know what you mean."

"You soon will. I've seen the pair of you and the 'FOR SALE' notice."

"So? It's my house. I can do what I like with it…and don't you dare go near him!"

"I'm not bothered about him, poor sod. Just another notch for you, eh? And I expect you've been through half the dick in that place, for starters," he said, pointing at the Leisure Centre across the car park.

"So? What's it to you?"

"Admit it, do you? You just used me, you conniving little tart."

"And you used me, Andy, don't forget. You loved it. You got your fair share of me and of everything else."

"That's just it. I didn't. You owe me."

"I don't owe you a penny."

"I'm going to get a lot more than that, Jan, before I've finished, I promise you."

"You do anything and you'll be back inside in five minutes flat."

"You're absolutely right, darling. But you'll see, you little piece of shit, you'll see."

Andy pushed her onto the car boot and stormed off. Although Janice was glad that he'd left her in one piece, she was scared to death and stared after him, wondering what the hell he was going to do.

*

Inside the Leisure Centre, Crowther and Harper had paid for their squash court and were in the changing room getting ready for their game. Crowther had told his friend about the fracas with the thermometer and about how he had to buy a new one, not forgetting the story of how he had got it home, of course.   After sharing a laugh, Harper was intrigued as to the reason why Allyson had to take her temperature in the first place.

"Because that's what the doctor told her to do," said Crowther, carefully draping his trousers over a hanger.

"Fair enough, but what's taking her temperature got to do with anything?"

"Well, when it changes, either up or down, I'm not exactly sure, that's when she starts ovulating. You know, eggs arrive or...something like that. Anyway, that's the time to...well, you know...that's the time."

"Ah, gotcha.   You mean that's when you're supposed to drop everything and get in there."

"Yes, thank you, Ian. Very nicely put."

Crowther pulled up his shorts and got his squash shirt out of his sports bag.

"I never knew that," muttered Harper. "You see me and Mary, well, we just used to get on with it, you know, never gave it a second thought. We had two of the little buggers end to end, called it a day and I had the snip - Bob's your uncle."

"Yes, I know, you've told me many a time. Trouble with us is that we've been trying for over a year now. It really started when her sister, Laura, had her second. Since then, not a sausage, so Allyson went to see the quack and he put her on to this temperature lark."

"But it doesn't work?"

"Not as yet. Every month she gets all excited and then…nothing."

"Must get you down, lad."

"Not half, I can tell you. As for her, well, it's getting to the stage where she can't even bear to say the words. She just leaves an open packet of Lillets by the bathroom cabinet to give me a clue. Never says a word."

"Don't you worry, Colin, just keep at it. It'll happen."

"Aye. That's what they all say."

"And if it doesn't: get her a dog."

"A dog? What the hell for?"

"It's a well-known fact - gives them something to mother. That'll take the edge off her appetite, you mark my words."

"You are a cynical old devil, you know."
"Takes one to know one."
"Aye. Maybe you're right."
They finished changing in silence.

CHAPTER FOUR

Sunday, August 11th, 1991: 10.10am

The Pemborough Kingdom Hall of Jehovah's Witnesses was situated to the south of the city in a quiet suburban street. Like most of the world's Kingdom Halls it was a fairly non-descript building, deliberately more functional than fashionable. There was certainly no external evidence of it being a church, which strictly speaking it was not, nor any internal evidence of worship, which didn't really happen. The building was, in fact, simply a meeting place, where the principal activity was Bible study and, in particular, the search to identify texts that backed up the Jehovah's Witnesses' beliefs, which they had based on those texts in the first place. The lack of any religious paraphernalia was more than made up for, it has to be said, by the intensity of that somewhat circuitous study.

All of that was what DC Collins came away with after her initial enquiries into the Jehovah's Witnesses' movement and into trying to contact the two men who had been seen leaving Sir Harold's house. Like many a born-again agnostic, she was sceptical to the point of scorn about any religion that insisted on interpreting any given Biblical text as incontrovertible proof of the validity of its own beliefs. Having said that, Collins was not so bigoted as to dismiss out of hand those beliefs nor anyone who held them: she just didn't believe them herself and often wondered how on earth anybody else could. She was pondering on the fact that wars had been fought over such apparently insignificant religious differences, as she looked up at Kingdom Hall from the passenger seat of a marked police car.

The car, with its police driver, had been parked outside Kingdom Hall for a good hour or more, and Collins was giving up hope of anyone coming along to 'open up', or whatever Jehovah's Witnesses did to signify that they were in business. The uniformed police driver shuffled in his seat, he was getting a numb bum, and turned over yet another page of the News of the World. He had read all that the paper had to say about Saddam Hussein and the Allies repelling of his invasion of Kuwait, which, quite frankly, wasn't a great deal, and was turning to the much more important issue of rising temperatures and sexual impropriety among MPs and bishops (was there a connection?), when Liz Collins decided that she'd had enough of waiting.

"I'm going to have one last look around and then that's it," she said, as she got out of the car and went up the steps to the front door of the building. She read the notice board for what seemed like the tenth time and looked up and down the street in search of anybody who could conceivably help her. There was nobody in sight. She returned to the car and got in, slamming the door.

"They should be here according to their meeting times: Wednesday at seven; Sunday at ten. Well, it's past ten already and it's Sunday, so where are they?"

"Doesn't look promising, I'll give you that," said the driver, folding up his paper.

"You're not wrong."

"So, can we get moving, 'cos I've read this rag cover to cover, and I'm about to lose all feeling in my left buttock."

"What a lovely thought. Go on, then. Let's call it a day and try again tomorrow. And pass us the News of the Screws, if you've finished with it. I need a bit of culture."

The driver stifled a laugh, started up the car and pulled away, heading for the Police Station in Priory Street. There was hardly any traffic to contend with, as they drove towards the city centre. In the distance, the driver caught a glimpse of the Cathedral spire, just as its bells started to toll, summoning the faithful.

*

In the Crowthers' bedroom, the Cathedral bells could also be heard, but a good deal louder: not so much summoning the faithful, as waking the dead. Allyson put down the thermometer and chart she had been looking at and snuggled up to Crowther, who had stirred at the noise of the bells and had lazily turned over with his back to her. She kissed the back of his neck and her hand slid down under the duvet.

"Who's that?" muttered Crowther, sleepily.

"Who do you want it to be?"

"What if I said…Cindy Crawford?"

"With what I've got in my hand, sunshine, you wouldn't dare."

"Ow! Why don't you cut your nails? Go back to sleep."

"The chart says it's the right time…for baby-making," whispered Allyson into his ear, as she pulled herself closer.

"Oh, it does, does it? Come on, you know I'm not an early riser."

"Oh, I don't know. Feels promising to me," said Allyson, with a smile on her face.

Crowther sighed, "Have you got the tissues?"

"You've not finished already, have you?"

"Shut up. And come here."

Crowther turned to face her, and they kissed passionately, his hands gently moving down her body.

"Mmm," he said. "What's that smell?"

"Me, I expect.'"

"You haven't, have you?"

"No, I haven't! It's my perfume, dickhead."

"Funny name for a perfume. Dickhead."

"Actually, it's Shalimar by Guerlain, and I've nearly run out, if that's of any interest. Do you like it?"

"Oh, yes, I like it all right."

At that point in the proceedings conversation more or less ceased and was replaced by a series of pleasurable moans and groans. The whole exercise was moving inexorably towards its climax, with Allyson becoming more and more vocal, when the front doorbell started ringing, loud and long.

"Oh, no! Who the hell's that on a Sunday morning?" moaned a breathless Allyson.

"I've no idea…Ian!"

"Ian? You've never called me that before."

"Shit! It's my fault. I asked him to pop round," said Crowther, leaping out of bed and throwing on some clothes. "Look, I'll set him to work in the garage. It's nothing complicated. I'll be back. Whatever you do…don't go away."

Allyson lay back on the pillows, sighing and shaking her head in good-natured disbelief, as Crowther stumbled across to the bedroom door, his trousers still round his ankles.

*

"You could have told me!"

"Oh, yes, terrific. And what was I supposed to say? - 'Don't turn up before half ten, Ian, as I'll likely be getting my leg over'."

They were standing at the bar of the Roebuck Pub, to where they had adjourned after the excitement of the morning.

"Colin, what was I supposed to think? It was embarrassing for a start, and then I thought she must be ill, what with all that moaning and groaning. How was I to know that you were at it?"

"Keep your voice down, will you?"

"Is she always like that when…"

"Shut it!"

"Sorry. Only you didn't seem to be contributing much - vocally."

"I'm the strong, silent type, and if you don't shut up about it, you'll find out just how…"

"I'm just saying."

"Well don't! You've said quite enough to be going on with, thank you very much."

Crowther had a long swig of his beer and took a moment to calm down.

"Anyway, after all that, she didn't suspect anything. I told her that you were sorting out a couple of dodgy bits of wiring for me."

"Good. All the garden lights are wired up and hidden in the garage, like you wanted. Just put them where you want them, and I'll drill a hole through the patio door later in the week, while she's at work. All you've got to do is feed the wire through, put a 13amp plug on it and you're in business. Think you can manage that?"

"I think so, yes. Cheers."

"I'll avoid her afternoon off, of course. That'll be Wednesday, if I remember rightly. Wouldn't want to disturb the Crowthers' naked lunch arrangement"

"Pack it in, you rotten sod," said Crowther, as Ian pointedly placed his empty glass on the bar. "That was your second pint, by the way, so that settles your wages for doing my electrics, and makes it your round. I'll have a pint of best and a packet of cheese and onion. Cheers."

Ian couldn't argue with that, so took out his wallet and tried to get the barman's attention.

CHAPTER FIVE

Monday, August 12th, 1991: 1.25pm

At the eastern end of Marine Parade, Brighton, East Sussex, and with magnificent views of the Channel, are some of the best examples of Regency architecture in the South of England. The Kemp Town estate, including Sussex Square, Lewes Crescent, and Arundel Terrace, was developed under the influence of the architects, Wilds and Busby, and contains many of the most impressive houses in the area.

Across the road from one of those houses, which had not as yet been turned into flats, was a marked police car. The driver and his WPC colleague had been waiting there for nearly two hours and were relieved when a taxi pulled up opposite them. They waited as the taxi's occupants, a man and a woman, retrieved a couple of items of luggage from the boot, paid off the taxi driver and went up the steps to the target house.

The man was just about to put his key into the mortice lock, when the police arrived at the foot of the steps.

"John and Anna Goodland?" asked the WPC.

The couple turned, reacted in surprise at the presence of the two police officers and looked at each other apprehensively, as if to say 'What's going on?'

"Yes," said John Goodland.

*

DC Liz Collins was again in one of the quiet suburban Pemborough streets, waiting patiently in front of Kingdom Hall. She had eventually managed to locate the Jehovah's Witnesses that the paper boy had seen leaving Sir Harold's house and had persuaded them to meet her and DCI Crowther. They had arrived promptly at two o'clock and were inside in the building's main office. Crowther had yet to appear, and Collins was becoming increasingly impatient, as it was by that time getting on for half past the hour.

Just as she was about to go into Kingdom Hall and apologise to the two waiting Witnesses, Crowther's car came careering round the corner and pulled up, a little too close for comfort she thought, behind Collins's rather beaten up Capri. Crowther leapt out of his car, locked it and set off towards the steps up to the building's open front door, followed by Collins.

"Where the hell were they?" he demanded, without any attempt at an apology for his late arrival.

"There was a weekend course in Leeds, and a whole load of them went up there. As a result, yesterday's meeting was cancelled. Our pair have just got back and came straight here."

"Sod's law, eh?"

"More like Jehovah's, sir."

"No doubt. Who have we got, then?"

"The older one is George Smithson, Jehovah's Witness all his life. The other one is some sort of trainee, as far as I could gather, called Conrad Brook. He's American but, funnily enough, he's quite normal."

"Liz! Mormon convert, is he?"

"Could be. He is wearing the regulation suit. Mind you, they all give me the willies."

"That's your father talking, that is," said Crowther, as they reached the open door. "Aren't we supposed to take our shoes off or something?"

"That's in a Mosque. They're in the office to the

right. But if you insist on kneeling down and facing Mecca, that's to the left."

"You should get a job as a guide, you know. Go on then, after you, show me where they are."

"Certainly. Walk this way, sir."

"If I could walk that way, I wouldn't need…"

"…the cream, doctor. Yes, thank you. We've heard it before. They're in here," said Collins, as she opened the door to the main office. They entered to find George Smithson and Conrad Brook, the Jehovah's Witnesses, seated behind a rather grand Partner's Desk. Crowther and Collins took the chairs opposite them.

"Afternoon, Mr. Smithson, Mr. Brook," said Crowther, nodding to each man in turn. "I trust I got that the right way round." He smiled and they both nodded back. "Good. First of all, thank you for coming in to meet us, and I'm sorry I was a bit late. Pressure of work. I'm sure you'll understand. I'm DCI Crowther - DC Collins you've already met. Now, this shouldn't take long…"

"What's this all about? Was it really necessary for you to meet us here?" said Smithson, who was obviously the senior of the two and was determined to assert his position. Crowther didn't rise to it and stayed calm throughout.

"It was either here or at the station. I thought you might prefer your home ground. After all, Mr. Smithson, we are conducting a murder investigation, and you were at the scene."

"You can't seriously think that we had anything to do with it!"

"I can think what I like, but what I want to know is what you did and what you saw. Now, after talking to the paper boy and his father, it seems pretty conclusive that it was you lads that the boy saw coming down the drive of Sir Harold Moorhouse's house sometime after five o'clock on Thursday last. Would that be right?"

"I've no idea."

"Yes, sir," offered Brook. "We were there, and it was ten after five. Our last call."

"Thank you, Mr. Brook. What happened when you were at the house?"

Smithson, whose irritation was palpable, responded, "The door was open. We rang the bell and called out. There was no reply, so we went away."

"Did you see anybody in the garden, or hear anything from in the house?"

"Nobody, and I've just told you there was no reply," said Smithson. "Presumably, whoever lived there had just left on his motorbike. People leave their doors open all the time, you know. The police should do something about it, they really shou…"

"You saw a motorbike?"

"Yes, sir," piped up Brook. "It came out of the drive."

"Sir Harold's drive?"

"Yes, sir."

"You're absolutely sure this motorbike came out of Sir Harold's drive?"

"Mr. Brook's just told you, hasn't he? It came out of the drive, as we were turning the corner."

'Thank you. Just making absolutely sure. Can you describe the rider?"

"He had a helmet on."

"Surprise, surprise. What colour and what was he wearing?"

"I've no idea."

"Mr. Brook?"

"It was a black helmet, I'm sure. His clothes? Didn't look like leather. Looked more like normal sort of clothing, and he was wearing shoes, I think, rather than boots."

Collins eased forward in her chair and asked, "Registration number?"

"Sorry, ma'am, no"

"Very well, what about the bike? Can you describe it, Mr. Smithson?"

"Describe it? Well…it was a motorbike."

"Yes, I think we've established that. Large, small, black, coloured?"

"The only thing I can remember was that it looked quite large, yes, and very powerful."

"That's what I thought," added Brook. "And it had a red gas tank on it."

"He means petrol tank."

"Thank you, Mr Smithson, I do speak fluent American."

"Really? And, for your information, I did notice that it had two shiny exhaust pipes, if that's of any use. They glinted as it disappeared."

"Going in which direction?"

"Errm…away from the centre of the village, would you say, Conrad?"

"Yes, definitely, away from the village, and fast, very fast."

"Is that all? We have things to do, you know." demanded Smithson, looking ready to get up and leave.

"Bear with us, Mr. Smithson, if you wouldn't mind. Believe it or not, we have 'things to do' as well, as I'm sure you appreciate. I'll put that description out, Collins. See if there's anything else these gentlemen can remember, then get back to the station. Thank you, Mr. Brook. Quite painless, wasn't it, Mr Smithson?"

Crowther left Collins to finish off the questioning and write up her notes. He didn't want to pin all his hopes on the sighting of a motorbike, but he knew that having something definite to follow up would give a much-needed boost to the whole inquiry.

*

At about the same time, Andy Davidson entered the Cathedral Centre shopping mall and consulted the index and floor plan of all The Centre's shops and stores. He found what he was looking for, glanced around to get his bearings and headed for the escalator.

*

"At least we've got something to look for, even if it is only a vague description of a motorbike and an even vaguer one of the rider," said Crowther, as he settled himself with a tea, and Collins with a black coffee, at an empty table in the canteen.

"I expect Superintendent Vance will be tickled pink, won't he?"

"Too true, Liz. He'll have a field day grabbing all the credit at the Press Conference. He records them, you know. Plays them back to his friends," said Crowther, taking a sip out of the chipped canteen cup.

"You are joking! What are they? 'Boys in Blue Movies'?"

"Something like that. Nice one!" Crowther laughed and nearly choked on his tea. "So, what are you doing with yourself tonight?"

"Sitting in front of the tele, I suppose."

"Not again. You watch too much, you know. You should be out on the pull."

"'Out on the pull'. Give it a rest. Anyway, where did someone your age pick up an expression like that?"

"Watch it! You're not getting any younger, either. Time marches on, you know."

"Ooh, we are trotting out all the olde worlde clichés today, aren't we? Besides, it's you who's taking your time, by all accounts…sir."

"Steady on, Detective Constable. We'll get there, one of these days. Anyway, I've already got a daughter, Helen. She may not be Allyson's, but she'll make me a grandfather before you're a mother."

"She's only twelve!"

"…going on twenty, and she's got some mouth on her, that girl, I can tell you. Yes, Trevor, what is it?"

Sergeant Trevor Beech had entered the canteen and spotted the pair of them. He had a fax in his hand and had walked over to Crowther.

"A motorbike, answering the description, such as it was, that we put out, was reported stolen from Brighton Railway Station on the day of the murder, sir. Brighton are talking to the owner as we speak. Registration number and details to follow."

"Crikey, that was quick. Somebody's on the ball. Thanks, Trevor."

"And there's a message from your wife, sir. She's expecting you home at six."

"Yes, yes, ok."

"Any later, could you give her a ring?" Trevor said, as he left them to it and went to get himself a tea.

"Do you know, I sometimes wonder what Allyson thinks I do all day. I'll swear she imagines that I'm going to drop everything in the middle of interrogating some murderer, and say 'Look, I'm terribly sorry, mate, but would you mind confessing? You see, if I'm not home by six, there'll be hell to pay at our house!'"

"I'm sure she thinks nothing of the kind…"

"Damn! I still haven't got her birthday presents!"

"Ouch! What are you going to buy her?"

"How the hell do I know? That's why I haven't got her anything."

"Have you ever thought of asking her what she wants? It'd be a start."

"I couldn't do that! It wouldn't be a surprise, would it?"

'True, but it'll be a wonderful surprise when she gets nothing, won't it? Hasn't she given you any hints? Women are famous for dropping them, aren't they? All right, all right, I'll rephrase that."

"Very wise. Now I come to think of it, she did mention black trousers and perfume the other day."

"There you are then! Good for you! Most men wouldn't recognise a hint if it got up and bit them."

"Yes, I suppose so. The thing is, I was hoping to get her something really original, but all I've come up with so far is a lawn-mower and a dog!"

Collins stared at him blankly, shook her head and went back to the safety of her tea.

*

Bourton Sports Equipment, one of Pemborough's premier sports goods shops, witnessed by its prestigious position opposite the main central escalators, stretched the full length of The Centre's mezzanine floor. It catered for every sportsman's requirements, from boot laces to top of the market skiing goggles. Neither of those was of interest to Andy Davidson, however, as he searched the depths of the store for exactly what he wanted. It didn't take him long to find it. The rather attractive assistant took his money, wrapped up his purchase and placed it in a Bourton Sports Equipment plastic bag.

"There you are, sir. Hope you win," she said, smiling, as she passed the bag to Andy.

"No doubt about it. I'll win all right," Andy smiled back, winked and left the store. He was well pleased with himself and with his plan, which had by now matured and had become fully formed in his devious and revengeful mind. With Stage One of it under wraps, as it were, he checked the time and set off towards The Roebuck to celebrate and go over the finer details of Stage Two.

*

Later that afternoon, in the Pemborough CID office at Police HQ in Priory Street, DC Collins was engrossed in a telephone call, while Sergeant Trevor Beech was reporting to Crowther.

"Banbury?"

"Yes, sir," confirmed Beech, "Banbury Railway Station car park. The parking attendant says the bike must have been parked there around 5.20pm last

Thursday, the day of murder. He swears it wasn't there at 5.15pm when he knocked off for the day, because if it had been, he'd have checked it for a ticket. But after he had got changed out of his uniform and was on his way home at 5.25pm, as usual, that was when he saw it. Also, it was still there on Friday, so he stuck a penalty notice on it at 9.30am, another at 3.30pm and went off early for the weekend. When it was still there this morning, he eventually phoned the local lads, and they've just this minute got on to us."

"And it's the same as the motorbike that was stolen from Brighton, and the same as the one that came out of Sir Harold's drive last Thursday?"

"Appears to be exactly the same, sir. Red tank, twin chrome exhausts, big job. It's the one all right, I'd put money on it. One of the locals is on his way to get confirmation of all the details and the registration number, as we speak."

"Good. Let's suss out the owner and see what Forensics have to say."

DC Liz Collins called across the room, while pointing at the phone in her hand, "Sir! Brighton CID on the line. Is it OK if John and Anna Goodland come up this evening and stay at Sir Harold's house?"

"Fine. We've got what we need. Oh, Liz! Since they're going to be up here, tell the Goodlands that I'll be round in the morning. About eleven."

"Right, sir."

As Collins went back to her phone conversation, DS David Banks entered the CID room with a file of papers and crossed to Crowther.

"This will interest you," he said, opening the file.

"What will?"

"A copy of Sir Harold Moorhouse's bank statements. Until two months ago, he was paying out cheques for either £5 grand or £10 grand at monthly intervals. Been going on for about two years. Clocked up just shy of a quarter of a million quid.

"Was he now?"

Crowther scanned the copy statements, noting where Banks had ringed the regular payments.

"Yes, I see what you mean. Bit steep for a standing order to the Readers Digest, isn't it?"

"I was actually thinking more like blackmail, sir."

"What? And the blackmailer caves his head in? It's a distant thought, I suppose, but why kill the goose?"

"Maybe because Sir Harold had had enough. Perhaps he threatened to expose the blackmailer and come to us. It would be motive enough to kill him. Depends what it was all about, of course, but well over two hundred grand and counting? It wasn't going to stop there, I'll bet."

"Perhaps not, but if your theory is correct those cheques would have had the blackmailer's name written all over them, wouldn't they? What does he do for an encore? Take Access?"

"They could have been made out to cash. Might have been a brown envelope job, with not a name or receipt in sight. You never know, sir."

"True. And it is odd, I grant you, someone taking out such big amounts on a regular basis. OK, you're on. Wouldn't be a bad idea to get the returned cheques from the bank, anyway, and if those are for cash, you might be in business, though I'm not entirely convinced, I must say."

"I'll get straight onto it, sir," Banks proudly announced and reached for the phone.

"Right, that's me away," said Crowther, grabbing his jacket on the way out.

"Oh, by the way, sir, Moorhouse Engineering have a very twitchy Managing Director, Graham Kirk. Nervous is putting it mildly."

"Oh, yes? What about competition, David?"

"Non-starter. Seems all Sir Harold was working on was the gearbox for John Goodland's racing car. Mutual passion apparently. Apart from that - nothing."

Crowther had his jacket on and was heading for the door.

"So, if your blackmail theory's going to work, it looks like something personal."

He stopped and turned to Banks.

"All right, fair enough, you go for it, David. I'll see what the Goodlands have to say in the morning...I'm off."

Crowther finally managed to leave, as Banks picked up the phone and dialled.

*

In the bedroom of the Crowthers' house, Allyson had just finished putting on her sexiest underwear and high heels. She was really quite pleased with the result of her efforts and was sure that it would have the desired effect. She was admiring herself in the Cheval mirror in the corner of the room, when the front door slammed.

"Ali! Allyson?" Crowther shouted out from the hallway.

"I'm up here. Got something to show you," she giggled as she said it.

"Hang about. Do you want a cup of tea?"

"Not at the moment, thanks. Up here, quick!"

She could hear his footsteps on the stairs, and she prepared herself for him to enter the bedroom. Just as she had decided on the most provocative pose she could think of, the phone rang.

"I'll get it," Crowther shouted, his footsteps retreating back downstairs.

Allyson sighed, looked at her reflection in the mirror and spent the next few minutes repositioning herself into an even more alluring pose.

"It's all right," said Crowther, ascending the stairs for the second time. "Wrong number, would you believe!"

He entered the bedroom and saw Allyson in full regalia. Words very nearly failed him and all he could manage was: "Fuck me!"

"You smooth talking bast...all right, if you insist."

"We only did it yesterday. Well, sort of."

"'Sort of' is about right, and with your friendly local electrician, Ian, prowling around in the garage, not exactly ideal, was it?"

"Granted," conceded Crowther, "and the poor lad didn't even finish."

"Neither did you, as I recall."

"Steady on! Anyway, isn't it too late for an encore?"

"Not necessarily. There's always a chance. Come here."

He went to her and they embraced. He ran his hand down her back, under her panties and over her buttocks. She slid her hand slowly between his legs and looked up at him.

"Is that nice?"

"Oooh, yes, that's nice. You do know City are playing ManU tonight, don't you? It's on the tele in ten minutes."

"If you're a good boy, I might let you watch the second half."

"The way I'm feeling at the moment, I'll be downstairs in time for the kick-off!"

"No, you won't. I think I can keep you hanging on a bit longer than that."

"I don't doubt it. By the way…"

"Mmm?"

"Before you get too carried away, what's for dinner?"

"Shut up. So, how do you want me?"

"Standing up in a hammock, I don't care."

They eased themselves onto the bed and proceeded to finish off what they had started the day before.

David Roper

CHAPTER SIX

Tuesday, August 13th, 1991: 11.00am

Anna and John Goodland, Sir Harold Moorhouse's daughter and son-in-law, had travelled up to Oxfordshire from their house in Brighton the previous evening. They had decided that they should be on hand at Sir Harold's house to deal with all the inevitable ramifications of a sudden death, not to mention giving the house the once-over with a view to either flogging it or eventually taking up permanent residence.

Anna was one of those women who know just how much, or rather just how little, make-up to use in any given circumstance. That morning, in anticipation of a visit from the police, which they had been informed of, she had opted for the 'natural look'. Added to her white cotton blouse, black pencil skirt and high heels, it succeeded in giving her the perfect mixture of grief and glamour that she intended. The fact that she was absently leafing through a Next catalogue, without a care in the world, would have told anyone watching, although nobody was, that she had more interest in her next Next purchase than with the loss of her father. But that was Anna all over. She looked out on a world that revolved entirely around her, and even her husband's boring racing car obsession and Sir Harold's untimely death were mere irritants to the settled state of her spoilt and selfish existence.

John, on the other hand, was driven by an ambition to move on. Although he lived on an island of self-interest, much like Anna, he did at least see himself escaping and having to work his way up the Formula 1 hierarchy of millionaire drivers. Anybody or anything that could help to fulfil that ambition was fair game and ripe to be exploited. But that was John all over, which made him and Anna such a contradictory, yet strangely complimentary, couple.

On that particular morning, he was engrossed in Sir Harold's design of a revolutionary gearbox for his racing car. The drawings were spread out on a coffee table in front of the lounge fireplace, to the right of which was a large TV, currently showing a local news programme. The TV announcer was coming to the end of the international part of the bulletin, and was about to turn to local matters, for which the Goodlands were eagerly waiting.

'...and the United Nations Security Council has called for an easing of the recent global trade embargo.

In other news, the search for the killer of millionaire engineer, Sir Harold Moorhouse, who was brutally murdered at his Oxfordshire home last Thursday, took a step forward today...'

"About time, say I," declared Anna, looking up from her catalogue.

"Shush, woman!"

"Don't you 'woman' me, John Goodland. They better get whoever it was."

"Yes, let's hope so, dear. Now, be quiet, there's a love."

John was trying to concentrate on the TV announcer, who was still on the same news item.

'...and our chief crime correspondent, Paul Stoddard, has this report.'

The TV changed shot to him standing outside Pemborough Police HQ in Priory Street.

'Police have been baffled, so far, by the apparently motiveless killing of one of the Engineering Industry's most respected figures...'

"And what are they doing? Nothing, it seems. I'll give them 'baffled!'"

"For God's sake, Anna, will you please…" as their voices got raised, and before the crime correspondent could impart any further information, the front doorbell rang, "…and who the hell's that!"

John leapt up and went along the hall to the front door. Anna continued her tirade at the TV.

"They better get whoever it was," she yelled, as she went to fix herself a vodka and tonic from the supply of drink on the sideboard and turned back to the TV.

'…however, a statement of the current situation was made, and an update…,'

In the meantime, John Goodland had opened the front door and come face to face with Crowther and DC Collins.

"Mr Goodland? DCI Crowther, DC Collins, Pemborough CID. May we have a word?"

"Yes, of course. We were expecting you. Please come in."

"Thank you."

"My wife's in the lounge. Come through, please."

The group went along the hall and into the lounge. Anna, nursing her drink, had settled herself into a large armchair. She made no attempt to get up or even recognise that they had entered the room. She stared at the TV.

'...at the Police Press Conference earlier today...'

"It's the police, Anna," said Goodland, quite emphatically, in an attempt to raise some element of politeness from her. She didn't respond.

From the TV came the unmistakable tones (unmistakable to Crowther and Collins, that is) of Chief Superintendent Vance, speaking at the Press Conference.

'Absolutely.   I'm pursuing a certain line of inquiry with the vigour you would expect in the circumstances, and I will release my findings when the time is right. I have...'

Crowther and Collins stared at the TV and exchanged a look. Before they could raise their eyes at any more of Vance's statement, Anna turned off the TV with the remote.

"The police, eh?"   said Anna.   "Still 'baffled', are we?"

"Good morning, Mrs. Goodland. I'm Detective Chief Inspector Crowther, this is Detective Constable Collins. We just need to ask a few..."

"Have you got him?"

"Not yet, I'm afraid, but we are progressing."

"Progressing? And what's that a euphemism for, Chief Inspector?"

Crowther risked a quick look to Collins, who returned it with a wry smile, as if to say, 'Hello, we've got one of those, have we?' Crowther nodded, sagely.

*

The Pemborough branch of the County Bank was situated in Market Street adjacent to the Cathedral and next to the ironically named Almshouse Mansions. The bank's three-storey Victorian building had been purpose built to house such a business, with offices on the first floor and a further floor for storage, which had recently been taken over by a firm of Accountants. The whole structure was built of local stone, and the tiled floors at ground level gave anybody who innocently wandered in the feeling of being inside a very large and well-kept Victorian toilet.

None of that feeling was appreciated by DS Banks, though, as he entered the bank and crossed to the enquiry desk. His thoughts were on the job in hand. As there was nobody behind the counter, he pressed the button marked 'Ring for Service', and somewhere in the bowels of the back office a bell sounded. A few minutes later, Allyson Crowther appeared.

"Hello, David! This is a pleasant surprise. Come to open an account?"

"Afraid not, Mrs Crowther. I've got an appointment with your manager. Official business."

"Oooh! Sounds serious. I'll tell him you're here. Have a seat."

Allyson disappeared into the back office. Banks sat down on one of the collection of wooden chairs, which looked for all the world as if they had been there since the place was built and, in all probability, they had been. Banks opened his newspaper and settled himself in for what he guessed might be a fairly long wait.

*

In the lounge of Sir Harold's house, Crowther and Collins were struggling to keep their tempers with Anna Goodland, who was proving to be about as helpful as a dose of flu to a dying man.

"John has just told you, hasn't he? We left Brighton on the 2.15pm train to Manchester. How many more times?"

"Why Manchester?" asked a somewhat tight-lipped Crowther.

"Not that it's any of your business but, if you must know, it was John's birthday at the weekend. If you want proof of that, his passport is in the top left-hand drawer of the sideboard. To answer your question, Chief Inspector: we decided on Manchester because that's where we met...oh, God, I can't believe we were up there enjoying ourselves while my father was lying in there...oh, God." sobbed Anna, breaking down in tears.

"I know, sweetheart, I know," said Goodland. "It's unbelievable that anybody could do...that to him. He must have..."

"Oh, John, don't, please."

"Sorry, my love."

"We'll find whoever it was, Mrs Goodland," Crowther tried to sound as confident as he could, but it sounded hollow, even to him.

"You'd better," said Anna, somewhat recovering her composure.

"Of course."

After a short pause, Crowther changed tack to what he felt was a more conversational approach and asked, "Your dad was quite well off, I understand."

"Yes, father was."

"Quite. Do you have any brothers or sisters we can contact for you?"

"No, I don't, and before you ask: yes, everything comes to me, since that's what you're hinting at."

"Not at all. Just getting things clear, Mrs Goodland; getting things clear. Did your father have any enemies; any business rivals, who might have held a…"

"Don't be ridiculous. Of course not. Everybody liked him."

"Well, somebody didn't, apparently."

"Bit uncalled for, Inspector, don't you think?" Goodland butted in.

"Mrs Goodland," Collins butted in, having decided it was about time she took over, although her question hardly improved the atmosphere. "To your knowledge, was Sir Harold involved in anything, or with anybody, that he might have preferred to keep private?"

"What's this woman trying to suggest?" demanded Anna, turning to face Crowther.

"DC Collins isn't suggesting anything, Mrs Goodland. She is simply trying to explore the full picture."

"Odd way of going about it, if you ask me: suggesting he was up to no good."

Crowther was about to open his mouth again, when a helpful look from Collins silenced him. He settled for a moment, quietly seething, while he tried to force himself to calm down.

*

The Manager's office at the County Bank gave DS Banks the feeling that he was back at school and had been summoned to the Headmaster's study. The room smelt of old books and furniture polish, with just a hint of cigar smoke, and the Manager's pin-striped suit and bow tie had a distinctly Dickensian feel about them.

When he had phoned earlier in the day, Banks had asked the Manager to dig out all the returned cheques drawn on Sir Harold Moorhouse's account for the past two years. In particular, he needed to know the identity of the payee, or payees, named on the cheques for £5 thousand and £10 thousand pounds, which had been paid out so regularly each month during that time. That information might well offer a significant lead in the murder investigation.

The Manager, an efficient character of the old school, duly produced several piles of Sir Harold's returned cheques and placed them on his desk. He had, rather helpfully, extracted the cheques for £5 grand and £10 grand, and had put them into chronological order, starting exactly two years ago.

"Just the cheques for £5 thousand and £10 thousand pounds, that's all you wanted, wasn't it?"

"Yes, thank you, sir," stuttered Banks, still feeling as if he was facing the Headmaster. "If you don't mind, that is."

"Not at all. Glad to be of assistance, as they say. As a matter of fact, my father was in the police. Got to be Assistant Chief Constable of Derbyshire, but that would be before your time, I suppose."

"Probably."

"Yes, certainly, I would think. Now, let's have a look at these cheques. You're interested to see who was the payee and/or payees or alternatively, if they were all payable to cash, I understand," he said, as he expertly flicked through them. "Well, no...no...no. None payable to cash, by the look of it. Interestingly, though, they are all made out to the same company, namely Portland Machines Limited. Yes, the same...the same...the same. The lot, it seems. Sorry to disappoint."

"No, that's interesting. Portland Machines Limited, you say. Mean anything to you?"

"Never heard of them. If I were you, I'd get onto Companies House in London. They'll have all the details: Directors, Shareholders, Accounts, the lot. Got the address here somewhere and the phone and fax number," he said, as he rummaged in a desk drawer.

"That's OK, sir. I can get all that information when I get back to the station. Thank you for your help. I have to get on now, so I'll send somebody round to collect all the returned cheques later. I really better get back with this information. Thank you again."

Banks shook hands with the Manager and made a quick exit.

*

It was a rare occasion indeed when Crowther 'lost it', but Anna Goodland was the kind of creature who could try the patience of a Saint, and Crowther was no Saint, so he 'lost it'.

"Let's put it this way, shall we? Was your father on the fiddle, or was he sexually active where he shouldn't have been?"

In the short silence that followed, everybody was frozen to the spot, awaiting the explosion that they all knew would inevitably follow Crowther's question. When the stunned occupants of the room had thawed out, all eyes turned towards Anna.

"How dare you!" she duly exploded, the sound she emitted being almost operatic in its volume and intensity.

Collins was as shocked as anybody at the way Crowther had behaved and realised that she was the only person who could stop the situation deteriorating into some kind of horrendous slanging match. Anna and Crowther were squaring up to each other, as Collins stepped in to referee the bout.

"What he means," she said decisively, dispensing with Crowther's police title and reducing him to the level of a mere mortal, "is that there are certain areas we need to eliminate from our inquiries. In order to eliminate them, we need to be assured that they never existed in the first place, and to do that there are certain questions we have to ask, including, unfortunately, those of a somewhat personal nature. However, they are merely questions, not conclusions or opinions. Therefore, you, in turn, can be assured that in asking them there is absolutely no accusation, or implied accusation, of any misconduct of any kind on the part of your late father, merely a request for information and clarification."

As a piece of diplomacy, Collins' intervention was masterful, and would have guaranteed her a place in any Middle East or Northern Ireland peace initiative.   Crowther recognised this and was both relieved and amused by her tactics.

"That is exactly what I meant to say, of course. Carry on, please."

"Thank you, sir. For instance, Mrs Goodland, if your father had fallen victim to, say, blackmail, we would have to try to determine…"

"Blackmail? Why do you think that? What have you found out?"

"Nothing, and we don't think that, necessarily. It was only an example."

At that moment, and conveniently, since Anna was getting worked up again, the house telephone rang. John Goodland answered it.

"Hello….yes, speaking…who's tha…yes, he is. Very well, hold on. It's for you Chief Inspector. A Sergeant Beech," said Goodland, tersely, handing the phone to Crowther.

"Thank you," he said, took the phone and turned to the window. "Crowther…yes, Trevor, what is it?" he listened, as Beech gave him the latest news. It was an update on the stolen motorbike that had since been found in the car park at Banbury Railway Station. When Forensics removed the three penalty notices from the motorbike, underneath they found an all-day pay-and-display ticket for Oxford station car park, timed at 10.07am on the day of the murder. "Thanks, Trevor. We're on our way. Get everybody on the team together at...two o'clock." He put the phone down and turned to the group, who were all watching him expectantly. "We have to go. Thank you so much for your help."

"Something actually happened at last?" Anna was smirking, back in Anna-mode.

"Indeed. How very astute of you," Crowther was condescending, back in Crowther-mode. "It's none of your business, of course, but if you must know, it's a serious parking offence. We'll keep you informed."

Crowther and Collins left the room, went down the hall and out of the front door.

"Useless, the lot of them," bleated Anna.

"Yes, dear," agreed John, simply because it was the easiest thing to do.

"I notice you didn't have much to contribute," she said, accusingly.

"You seemed to be doing quite well without me, dear. As usual."

John smiled at her, indulgently, and went back to studying the plans for his new gearbox. Anna seized her copy of the Next catalogue and threw it at him.

*

"A right little bundle of joy she turned out to be!"

"To be fair, sir, her father has just been brutally murdered."

"Yes, yes, I know. It's probably me."

"Probably, sir." Collins said with a smile.

"Liz! Well done, by the way, getting me out of the sh…you know what I mean."

"Sir."

She was driving them back to Priory Street HQ. As he didn't want to drive, Crowther had claimed tiredness. In reality, he wanted to think, and he rubbed his eyes and yawned.

"Heavy night?" asked Collins.

"No," he said, a little too quickly, as he remembered what he and Allyson had got up to. "Not in that sense."

"I see, I think. In exactly what sense was it a heavy night, then, may I ask?"

Crowther needed a change of subject, and fast. He did his best.

"It was…nothing. What did you think of the Goodlands?"

"Penniless, ambitious hunk weds rich, spoiled brat."

"Ha-ha! You'd do well as a sub-editor, you know. You have this knack of reducing the most apparently innocent situation to its most shockingly sordid basis. I like it."

"You agree, then?"

"Yes, I agree. All is not well in the house of Goodland. Not quite sure what is 'not well' with them, but I reckon ambition and over-indulgence are just the tip of the iceberg, if that's not too much of a mixture of terms."

"I get the picture. I reckon there's a lot more to John and Anna Goodland than meets the eye."

Crowther had the utmost respect for Liz Collins' opinion. Not only on the grounds of female intuition, which he actually believed in, but because Liz was the daughter of his old friend Frank and was heir to the Collins' family flare for detective work.

In the early days, the then PC Colin Crowther and PC Frank Collins had been inseparable, and it hadn't taken long for the powers-that-be to realise their potential. They had both quickly moved into CID, and together were a formidable team.

When it came, the tragedy was all the greater for their closeness.

Twenty years previously, working undercover, Frank had infiltrated a somewhat insalubrious gang, who were engaged in the charming business of pandering to the proclivities of those who preferred their sexual partners to be well under the age of consent. With a six-year-old daughter of his own at home (Liz), Frank had perhaps not been the ideally dispassionate choice of police officer to enter into the murky world of child sex abuse. To say that his domestic situation tended to cloud his otherwise impeccable professional judgement was an understatement. He found the whole business nauseating and would have cheerfully strung up the lot of them himself.

On the night of the raid, Crowther was part of the armed unit that went in at the rear of the building where the gang was based. It was a detached house in half an acre of ground. The front lawn ran down to the road, and was overlooked by most of the windows, but at the back there were trees and bushes for cover.

The plan was that one of the rear assault group of six should cause a disturbance in the back garden, as if some drunk had stumbled over the fence for a pee, say, thus drawing the gang away from the front. Seconds later the front assault group would burst through the front door, the remaining rear assault group would burst in at the back, and the gang would be sandwiched in between.

What Crowther didn't know, as he entered through the back door of the house, was that in the confusion following the 'disturbance', and strictly against orders (he had been told to keep well out of the way), Frank had disarmed the gang leader of their only gun. The leader realised what was happening, grabbed a knife from the kitchen table, and lunged at Frank. Frank was the quicker. He side stepped the knife, sent the leader sprawling with a kick to the groin, and although he would have preferred to put the bullet through the head, fired a warning shot that splintered the wooden flooring only inches from the man's right ear. Even in the heat of that moment his training had taken over.

Less than a second later Crowther's training also took over, and he fired into the darkness of the kitchen. He was shooting at what he thought was the leader of the gang, the only man who had a gun - according to the information supplied by Frank.

The subsequent Internal Police Enquiry exonerated Crowther of any blame for Frank's death. Crowther was not so generous to himself, and he never really got over it. When Frank's daughter, Liz, joined the force over thirteen years later, at the age of nineteen, Crowther did all he could to help and advise her. Understandably, his feelings of guilt had something to do with it, but it was without doubt that Liz Collins had the makings of a bloody good copper.

She had been told about the circumstances surrounding her father's death, and of Crowther's involvement, when she joined. Her intuition had led her to suspect something of the kind for a long time, so it was less of a shock than it might otherwise have been. However, a less strong-willed person might have been unforgiving, but Liz knew that her father would have reacted in exactly the same way had the positions been reversed in that house twenty years ago.

The result was that her relationship with Crowther had deepened over the years, and, although neither of them fully realised it, they had been brought closer together, as only those who share a common grief can be.

Crowther's phone rang and shattered his moment of nostalgia.

"Crowther," he mumbled, still half-immersed in the past. "Oh, hello, Donna. All right?" Donna, who was Allyson's best friend at the County Bank, where they had both worked for nearly a decade, took a deep breath, which Crowther heard and which told him that it was no social call.

"I'm fine, Colin. It's Allyson I'm worried about."

"What about her? What's happened?"

"She's in a bit of a state, that's all."

"What do you mean 'a bit of a state'? Has she been hurt?"

"No, no. Nothing like that. She's OK. It's just that I really think she needs to speak to you. She downed tools and rushed off for an early lunch at The Roebuck, but don't tell her I told you."

"Right. I'm on my way…"

Crowther turned off his phone and took stock of where they were on their journey back to Priory Street.

"…take the first left, Liz, and drop me by The Roebuck."

"What's the panic? Anna Goodland driven you to drink?"

"No, no. Don't know yet. I need to get to Allyson. Quick as you can."

"Thirty seconds, no less, sir," she said calmly, as she floored it and cut up an unsuspecting cyclist, who responded with the traditional single digit gesture.

Crowther hardly let the car come to a halt before he was out and heading for the pub. He was turning over all the possibilities in his head but couldn't settle on any one thing that would have made Allyson jump ship at such short notice. Liz Collins watched him disappear into the lounge bar, shrugged her shoulders and set off back to base, pursued vigorously by the angry and increasingly breathless cyclist.

*

Allyson was sitting by a window, nursing a glass of white wine and staring out at the world as it passed by. Engrossed as she was in her thoughts, she never noticed Crowther come in and stand behind her.

"Allyson,' he whispered quietly, then louder. "Allyson."

She turned at the sound of his voice, although her mind was miles away.

"Mmm?" she said, and slowly woke from her reverie. "Oh, hello. Where did you spring from?"

"Just passing. Are you all right?"

"I'm fine," Allyson lied and took a long swig of her drink.

"No, you're not," he told her and sat down. "What's the matter? Come on. Tell me."

"It's my sister."

"Lorna? What about her? Is she in trouble or something?"

"No, she's fine."

"Well, what? Allyson, you're freaking me out here. What is it?"

"She's pregnant again."

"Oh, no."

"Oh, yes. That'll be their second since we started trying. It's not fair."

"Bloody hell! You know what I mean. Great news, of course, but…how did you find out this time?"

"She phoned me at the bank about half an hour ago. I'm really pleased for her, for them both, I really am. It just gets…"

"I know. I know."

"It just gets to you for a minute, that's all."

"I know. They must be over the moon."

"Yes, they must. I start to wonder if we're just wasting our time, you know."

"Bollocks! It's early days yet."

"It's been over a year, Colin. I'll be thirty-five on Friday, and you're not getting any younger, are you?"

"How dare you! I've still got all my hair and most of my teeth."

"It's not your hair or your teeth I'm interested in!" Allyson smiled and relaxed a little.

"Steady on! Not in the pub."

"But you are old enough to be my father."

"I'm glad I'm not, though. I'd get arrested."

"So, you reckon you'd be up to playing football with a teenager when you're pushing seventy?"

"I reckon! As long as the wheelchair doesn't get a puncture, of course."

They both laughed and held each other.

"Listen, I know it's difficult, but worrying only makes it worse, you know. Tell you what, let's go out somewhere really nice for your birthday, eh? Daddy's treat," he said, smiling and kissed her.

"No, Colin. Look, I know you're right, but I want to be at home. Just us."

"Your wish is my…whatsit!…as they say. Whatever makes you happy. Have I got surprises for you, young lady?"

"There's only one surprise I'm looking forward to," she said, finishing her wine. "You do want us to have a baby, don't you?"

"If it's anything like you, it'll be a stunner. Another drink?"

Crowther immediately went to the bar, knowing full well that he hadn't actually answered her question.

*

The whole team had assembled in the CID office at two o'clock, as ordered by Crowther. Detective Sergeant David Banks, Detective Constable Liz Collins and a further Detective Sergeant and four Detective Constables (one female) were mooching around, most of them having just finished a hurried lunch. The general chatter, mostly about the fact that he was ten minutes late already, eased back to a fairly quiet murmur, as Crowther himself entered.

"Sorry I'm late, boys and girls," he said, placing a Marks & Sparks bag, containing Allyson's birthday black trousers (size 10, £35), on the floor and taking his position facing the team. The chatter had increased in volume, as the team took their seats or stood by the window.

"Right, settle down. Let's get back to work, shall we? Now, what do you make of this?" He turned over a large flip sheet resting on an easel next to the whiteboard.

"Is it a book or a film, sir?" Banks flashing his rank by daring to heckle the boss.

"Murder mystery, actually, if you must know." On the flip sheet was written:

MOTORBIKE SIGHTINGS

LOCATION	TIME	EVIDENCE
BRIGHTON:	6.45am	Owner parked it (stolen 7.00am)
OXFORD:	10.07am	All-day Pay-and-Display
MURDER SCENE:	5.10pm	Jehovah's Witnesses
BANBURY:	5.20pm	Parking Attendant

"Now listen," said Crowther, indicating each of his points on the flip sheet. "Our alleged killer steals a motorbike from Brighton railway station at around 7.00am…"

Banks raised his hand.

"No, DS Banks, you may not go to the toilet. However, to anticipate your question: the bike must have been nicked about then, because, as it says here, the owner parked it at 6.45am, so he would be in time to catch his train at 6.55am. More to the point, perhaps, is the fact that at that time of day it's got to take nigh on three hours to get to Oxford Railway Station, and we know the bike was parked there at 10.07am, because of the all-day pay-and-display ticket stuck on it. Therefore, it must have left around 7.00am. All agreed?"

General nods all round indicated their consent, so far. Crowther returned to pointing at the flip sheet.

"Right. Seven hours after that, at 5.10pm, God knows why the gap, the bike, ridden by our possible murderer, was seen leaving Sir Harold Moorhouse's house by the Jehovah's Witnesses, so we can take that as Gospel before Banks sticks his oar in."

"Sir." Banks accepted the dig and rode the laughter and jeering around him.

"Thank you. Thank you. Settle down. Around ten minutes after that, the bike was seen in the car park at Banbury Railway Station. Hands up anyone who can tell me what the hell I'm talking about."

Collins spoke up, "Sir."

"Oh, hello, here we go. Female intuition to the fore."

Crowther eyed the DC who had made the remark and butted in, "Don't knock it, Geoff. Anyway, I take it that it must have been male intuition that forgot to put the handcuffs on Harry Cawcroft. By the way, where is Harry now, Geoff. Any idea?"

Geoff, the guilty DC, looked suitably embarrassed, and physically crumbled under the weight of the guffaws emanating from the rest of the team. Crowther brought them all to order, "Thank you, everybody. Liz, you wanted to say something."

"Questions really, sir. Because of the all-day pay-and-display ticket at Oxford, timed at 10.07am, it's possible, even probable, that the killer didn't need the bike until late afternoon. That was when he, apparently, wanted to be at Sir Harold's house by five o'clock. But, as you said, why the seven-hour gap? Why such a long delay? It may be that he had to be somewhere else, or he had to appear to be somewhere else. Setting up an alibi, maybe. Also, his journey from Sir Harold's house to Banbury was done in just ten minutes. He must have been in one hell of a hurry to do it that fast. So, again why? Why the long delay, followed by the sudden hurry?"

"That's a lot of questions why, but not many answers," muttered Banks.

"True," said Crowther, "but there might be something there, you know. I mean, I get the bit about the delay possibly being used to set up an alibi. That's fine, as far as it goes. What I don't get is why the bike had to be left at Oxford Railway Station in the first place. Granted, it's near-ish to the murder scene, but so are lots of other places with untraceable free parking, and why does it end up in Banbury? More questions why?"

Banks stepped forward, deep in thought, raised his hand and spoke out, "Sir, perhaps one of the answers to all those questions is rooted in something that's staring us in the face."

The whole team turned to him.

"You see, apart from the murder scene, every time the bike appears it's in a car park."

Derisory mutterings and calls of 'So what?' came from the team.

"Yes, so what? Nothing unusual about that, I agree. However, all those car parks just happen to be attached to Railway Stations: Brighton (where the bike was stolen), Oxford (where it was parked all day) and Banbury (where it ended up). Why, you might say, did our killer choose or perhaps, more to the point, need the bike to be at one Railway Station or another throughout the day of the murder? Just a thought."

"Maybe, but it's a bloody interesting thought," said Crowther. "If we link the fact that the bike was at those Railway Stations with the theory that the killer was using that fact to establish some sort of an alibi, we might be able to join the dots up and make sense of it all. Yes…Railway Stations. The more I think about it, the more I like it. Good work, David. Right, to follow that up, I want the times of all trains to and from Brighton, Oxford and Banbury last Thursday and specifically times of trains around sightings of the bike. Plus, I want to know everything about anybody who bought any kind of ticket just after 10.07am at Oxford, and about 5.20pm at Banbury. Divide it amongst yourselves."

The whole team groaned.

"Come on, you must all have been train spotters in your time. Dust off your anoraks and get going."

The team huddled into twos and threes, as they went to leave the room. Banks approached Crowther.

"May I have a word, sir?"

"Sure. Let's go to my office."

As they walked along the corridor, Liz Collins caught them up on her way out. Banks couldn't resist a bit of a dig at her, "Drawn the short straw, eh, Collins?"

"Not at all. I've volunteered to do Oxford, and then some window shopping."

"What for? A dishy ticket seller?"

"Oh, grow up…sir," she growled at Banks.

"Stop it you two!" Crowther had raised his voice to stop the pair of them from bickering.

"Yes, sir," said Collins. She then dismissed Banks with a shake of her head and headed for the way out.

Crowther watched her go and, almost to himself, muttered, "She's wasted on her own, you know…"

"Don't look at me," said Banks. "Not my type."

"…and she's got her father's instinct. Bloody good copper, Frank Collins was."

"So I've heard," Banks nodded agreement, having listened to the Collins family's glowing references far too many times before.

"Right," said Crowther, getting back to business. "What did you want a word about?"

"Sir Harold's mystery cheques."

"What about them?"

"All paid to a company called Portland Machines Limited."

On their journey to Crowther's office, they had reached the drinks vending machine.

"Oh, yes?" Crowther paused and rummaged in his trouser pockets. "Have you got any change? I'm dying for a tea. Portland Machines, you say, eh? So presumably that means bye, bye to your blackmail theory."

"Looks like it. However, it means hello, hello to something else that's turned up. Here you are, sir."

Banks gave him some loose change. Crowther thanked him and carefully put several coins into the machine, "Great. Ta. Now, if I want tea, I have to press Hot Chocolate, she said. Right, here goes," he said cautiously, pressed the button and waited. "So, what's this 'something else' that's turned up?"

"Well, on the Bank Manager's advice, I got onto Companies House in London and they've just this minute faxed through a set of accounts and a list of directors of Portland Machines Limited."

"Quick off the mark."

"I do my best."

"Not you. Companies House. Those places usually take a week, at least."

"Yes, of course. Anyway, I'm not an accountant but, from the amount they've had off him, it seems fairly obvious that Sir Harold Moorhouse was Portland Machines' only means of support...since withdrawn."

"Enough for a motive?"

"If I remember rightly, the phrase is 'woolly thinking', isn't it? Why kill the goose?"

"David. Not a good idea to quote my perceptive remarks back at me, there's a good lad," said Crowther, taking the plastic cup from the drinks machine.

"Sir?"

"Never mind. Forget it..."

Crowther handed the cup to Banks.

"...and have a vegetable soup. You may as well, you paid for it," he tossed the remark over his shoulder as he set off towards his office. "So, what about Portland Machines' directors? Any joy there?"

"Yes, indeed, sir   Peter Feldman, solicitor. Graham Kirk, Moorhouse Engineering's twitchy Managing Director, if you recall…"

"Interesting."

"It gets better. And, wait for it, would you believe - John Goodland, Sir Harold Moorhouse's son-in-law."

"Mmm. The plot sickens, as they say."

"Even more sickening is the fact that Kirk has got a record for assault. Road rage. Beat up a motorist a couple of years ago over being cut up at a roundabout. Charming character. And, to top it all, this came over from Forensics," announced Banks, handing over a report form. "I had a feeling Mr Kirk wasn't kosher. I better have another word."

Crowther scanned the form, looked up and nodded his agreement, "I think you should."

*

The executive toilet suite at Moorhouse Engineering Limited was the best that money could buy. Furnished with floor-to-ceiling tiling, marble sinks and porcelain of the highest quality, it was rumoured to have cost more than the price of a Pemborough suburban bungalow. However, notwithstanding its undeniably expensive and classy construction, traditional toilet etiquette still demanded that men should stand side by side staring fixedly into the urinal bowls, which were ingeniously designed to deliver a fair proportion of each man's pee back and onto his shoes. Despite that, Tom Marchbanks, the Company Accountant, always rather enjoyed the elegant surroundings, and would linger there as long as possible, washing and drying his hands.

At that moment, however, he was still hunched over one of the urinal bowls, mid-pee, as the door behind him opened with a flourish, and Graham Kirk, the Managing Director, swept in, as only Kirk could, and took up the stall next to him. Once he had established an adequate flow, Kirk cleared his throat and said, "I think I owe you an apology, Tom. I was bloody rude last Friday."

Much as he wholeheartedly endorsed that admission, a somewhat tight-lipped Marchbanks politely replied, "That's OK," somewhat taken aback by the un-Kirk-like admission.

"No, I mean it. Really. I'd had a pig of a hellish long day: driving all the way from Brighton; hearing about Harold; lousy night's sleep. Sorry."

"I understand,' lied Marchbanks, fairly successfully hiding his unsympathetic feelings.

"Thanks. I appreciate you saying that. It's not everybody who would be so sympathetic, you know.

I really mean it, Tom. Yes, it's good to have friends who understand."

In an attempt to extricate himself from this bizarre volte face in Kirk's character and from what was becoming as near to a grovelling apology as Kirk was capable of, Marchbanks zipped up, moved to the sinks and turned on a tap. Kirk immediately followed and stood next to him again.

"Ah, there was one other thing..." he said, as if it had just come to him out of the blue.

"And what was that?" asked Marchbanks, warily, as he began washing his hands.

"Last Thursday...you...left about five, did you?"

"As usual, yes. Why?"

"It's nothing really. Normally, I wouldn't ask, you know me. It's just that...well, it would be doing me a great favour if you could say that you saw me in the car park as you left, say, about five...ish."

"Say it to whom?"

"Oh, you know, anybody who might ask."

They both went to dry their hands on the Egyptian towels provided.

"I see. Why not talk to your secretary? She'll verify your whereabouts, if you tell her to, I'm sure. Why involve me?"

"I don't think Miss Stannard would understand, Tom. She wouldn't, shall we say, get the message, if you know what I mean. It's more of a 'man' thing. Get my drift, eh?"

"Ah, of course, a 'man' thing. I think your drift is fairly obvious. I get it, loud and clear."

"Good man. Knew you would understand. Thanks. I owe you one."

"I look forward to receiving it," said Marchbanks, heading for the door and exiting. "You'll give my regards to your wife, I'm sure."

Kirk considered a reply, decided against it and followed him out of the door and towards the lift. At Reception, he saw DS Banks and a uniformed officer. To avoid them, he changed direction and was about to use the stairs, when Banks spotted him.

"Mr Kirk!"

Kirk turned, putting on his favourite welcoming smile, and crossed to Reception.

*

A man on the underwear and/or cosmetic floor of any large department store always lurks around looking for all the world like some incompetent, undercover trainee store detective. He looks around furtively at all the other customers, who are women, of course, studiously avoids the gaze of any assistants in the vicinity and, basically, sticks out like a sore thumb. His suspicious behaviour is largely ignored by the staff, who have seen it all before. They know that, eventually, he will give in and either make a dive for the most provocative-looking thong on show or, if he's on the cosmetic floor, choose something wholly inappropriate from the 'Beauty on a Budget' range, which costs less than half the price of a packet of fags.

Such a man was Crowther, as he struggled to look casual in the cosmetic department of Boots the Chemist on Market Square, Pemborough. He had often wondered why the assistants in these places seemed to be under orders to ladle onto their faces as much of the product they were selling as was humanly possible. It had occurred him on more than one occasion that their fixed smiles were probably there to hold the make-up in place and to prevent it from crumbling like Queen Nefertiti's death mask. But he was a man on a mission and dismissed those thoughts, as he struggled to understand what Donna, Allyson's best friend, was trying to tell him over the phone.

"Where are you now?" she asked

"Boots."

"Yes, I know that, but where in Boots?"

"Make-up, of course."

"Good. That's a start. Now, can you see a big, long display cabinet, with lots of different names above it: Yves St. Laurent, Chanel…"

"Ah! Got it. Now what?"

"You're looking for Guerlain."

"For what?"

"Guerlain," Donna repeated the name and then spelled it out. "G..U..E..R..L..A..I..N, Guerlain. OK?"

"OK, I'll have a look. What is it?"

"What do you mean, 'what is it?' It's a trade name, Colin. What you want is their perfume. It's called Shalimar. Ah! I've got to go. Allyson's coming over. Shalimar. Bye."

"What? Donna? Donna?"

Crowther switched off his mobile, wandered over to the display cabinet and tried to give the impression that he knew what he was looking for. He knew he had totally failed when, out of the corner of his eye, he spotted a smartly dressed female sales assistant making a beeline for him.

"Does sir need any help?" she said, smiling the predatory smile of one who knows a juicy prey when she sees one.

"Oh, hi. Yes, actually, I do. I'm looking for some…gwarelin, is it?"

"I think sir means Guerlain. It's just here."

"Right. Thanks a lot."

With a wave of his hand, Crowther turned towards the display, in the hope that the assistant would take the hint and continue her prowling elsewhere. No such luck.

"Any particular fragrance in the Guerlain range, sir?"

"Ah, now then, it's called…well, when she said it, it sounded like Shergar, but that can't be right, can it?' Crowther laughed, although, from her lack of reaction, this girl was no follower of the gee-gees.

"Shalimar, sir?"

"That's the fella!"

"Did 'madame' want the Eau de Toilette, Eau de Parfum or the Perfume?"

"What's the difference? Don't tell me! This is when you say twenty quid, isn't it?"

"I wish I could, sir. Fifty pounds is nearer the mark."

"What?"

"It rather depends on what sir wants."

"Sir hasn't got a clue, quite frankly. The Perfume, I suppose."

"Of course, sir. In the Guerlain, Shalimar Perfume range we start at 35, then 65, then 110."

"Those are the quantities, are they?"

"No, sir, prices."

"In pounds?"

"Yes, sir, in pounds. The quantities do double each time…"

"Pays to buy in bulk, then?"

"…and the Perfume is very long-lasting, sir."

"I should blo…thank goodness for that. OK, sold. I'll take it."

"So, the £35 Perfume for sir. If…"

"No!" Crowther cut her off, sounding hurt, as if going for the cheapest option were an outrageous suggestion. "Sir wants the £110 Perfume, thank you very much, and let's hope it lasts a lifetime."

"Of course, sir."

The assistant took the most expensive, yet the smallest, of the three Perfume boxes, and went to wrap it up. As she did so, DC Liz Collins entered the shop and crossed to Crowther.

"Sir!" said Collins.

"Drop the 'sir' please, I've had enough of it. Call me plain Colin, for goodness' sake."

"We've found John Goodland at last. He's out at Silverstone speed-testing his racing car."

"Great. I'll just see if I can get a mortgage to pay for this Perfume, and we'll be off."

*

"I wasn't there! How many more times?"

Graham Kirk, Moorhouse Engineering Limited's Managing Director, threw his arms up in despair. Across the desk from him sat DS Banks, who had returned with questions based on something that had recently come to light, although, for the moment, Banks wasn't letting on exactly what that 'something' was.

"So, where were you?"

Kirk sighed and repeated what he had already told Banks several times, "I spent Wednesday in Brighton at Portland Machines, stayed overnight at The Old Ship Hotel and drove back to Pemborough on Thursday."

"Yes. The hotel in Brighton confirmed that you checked out at 7.55am, and you told me that nobody saw you until you got back to your office later that afternoon. Around 6.00pm, didn't you say?"

"Yes, I did, although come to think of it, I seem to remember seeing Tom Marchbanks, our Accountant, in the car park as I was parking. He's always out of here bang on the dot of five o'clock is Tom, very punctual, so I must've got back earlier than I said. Around five, presumably."

"Presumably.   Nevertheless, what were you doing for the best part of twelve hours, Mr Kirk? Playing on Brighton Pier?"

"I've told you already, Sergeant. I walked along to the Marina, looked at the boats, they're an interest of mine, and then I walked back again. After that, I drove to Devil's Dyke. It's a local beauty spot that you should check out if you're ever down that way. Stunning views.   Anyway, I worked on business papers in my car and set off back to Pemborough at…oh, I don't know, midday, maybe a bit later."

"Did you eat at this…Devil's Dyke place?"

"No, I didn't. I'd had a large breakfast at The Old Ship before I left."

"Five hours to get to Pemborough? Give it a rest."

"Traffic, if you must know. It's two or three hours at best, and a foul-up on the M25 makes it anybody's guess."

"What did you use to kill him?"

The sharp change in tack didn't faze Kirk in the slightest.

"Oh, please, Sergeant, give it a rest, to use your words. I have not seen Sir Harold, or been anywhere near him, for more than a fortnight."

"Funny then that the papers we found on his desk, and dated the day of his death, have your fingerprints on them."

*

Jeremy Hartley-Jones wasn't exactly an Estate Agent. If truth be told, he wasn't an Estate Agent at all. He was, in fact, an undergraduate killing time, before returning to Manchester University, by showing prospective buyers around properties marketed by his father's firm of Pemborough-based Estate Agents.

On that particular day, Tuesday, 13th August, 1991, he was at Janice Holloway's house, Oakridge Lodge, Castle Avenue, Pemborough, and was doling out the old 'Estate-Agent-speak' to a potential buyer, as they emerged onto the patio.

"Yes, I agree, the triple aspect lounge is one of my favourite rooms, too," cooed Jeremy, although he had never actually set foot in the house until five minutes before. "If you'd care to step out here, you'll see that the property benefits from a quite stunning patio and pool area. To be honest, this property was under offer from virtually day one. Buyer withdrew, though. Lucky for you, eh? Now, this pool is irresistible, isn't it?"

"Irresistible," echoed the prospective buyer, as the pair of them stood at the edge of the pool, admiring the shimmering water and the view of the immaculate garden beyond. The buyer put his hand gently on Jeremy's shoulder, whispered, "Enjoy," into his ear, and pushed him in.

Jeremy resurfaced from his unscheduled dip, desperately trying to keep his mobile above water, and spluttered something unintelligible.

The buyer turned away and went back into the house. He picked up the parcel that he had brought with him, which he had left in the hall, and set off up the stairs to the first floor, taking them two at a time. There was something he was dead set on doing, and nothing was going to stop Andy Davidson from doing it.

*

While Andy was making his way upstairs towards Janice Holloway's bedroom, and Jeremy Hartley-Jones was dripping all over the patio, thirty-odd miles away, in Northamptonshire, on the eastern side of the M40 motorway, John Goodland was about to speed-test his prototype Formula 1 pride and joy at the Silverstone Motor Racing Circuit. Several mechanics were clustered round the car waiting, rather impatiently it seemed, for the 'off'.

Unfortunately for them, Goodland had been collared by DCI Crowther and DC Liz Collins, who had just arrived and were questioning him about Portland Machines' dependence on Sir Harold Moorhouse for its financial survival.

"Thick end of a quarter of a million quid, Mr Goodland? That's one hell of a lot of money to be throwing around," said Crowther, unable to disguise the irritation he always felt when dealing with the man.

"Yes, indeed it is, Inspector, but you must understand that my father-in-law was a very generous man and was in love with motor racing. However, regardless of his proclivities, I don't see that where he 'threw' his money, as you so uncharitably put it, has anything to do with you. You must excuse me," he made his condescending apology and started to get into the car.

Collins couldn't stand Goodland's attitude either and decided to stick her oar in, "Why did Sir Harold stop making payments to your company?"

"You'll have to ask him that, young lady."

"We tried, but understandably he's being a little uncooperative ...sir."

"Touche."

"But he did withdraw his financial support rather suddenly, didn't he!" Crowther offered it more as a statement than a question.

"Yes. 'Good old Harold' rather dropped us in it, I'm sorry to say."

"That must have been irritating. Did he give his reasons?"

"Not in so many words. He seemed to have gone off the whole idea."

"Or gone off you, perhaps." Crowther ploughed on before Goodland could respond to that rather personal remark. "Did your wife know that her father was paying such large amounts of money to you, via Portland Machines?"

"As a matter of fact, she didn't. She disapproves of me racing."

"Oh dear, what a shame, and I suppose that now she holds the purse strings, you're stuffed, aren't you?"

"Not at all. It's me she wants, not the money."

"I'm sure we all admire her taste." Crowther ended the verbal duelling by getting back to facts. "Where were you last Thursday?"

"You really are a little terrier, aren't you, Inspector? You know full well that I was in Brighton all morning and with my wife on the train to

Manchester all afternoon. I'm sure that you've already checked the train times."

"Yes, of course, the good old 2.15pm from Brighton."

Goodland settled himself into his car, ignoring them both, and proceeded to make preparations to drive off. Crowther and Collins exchanged a look and watched the car being pushed out of the Pits by the mechanics.

*

In the master bedroom of Janice Holloway's house in Castle Avenue, Andy Davidson was laying about him like a good 'un with the baseball bat that he had bought at Bourton Sports. He had demolished her dressing table and chair and was making short work of the mirror behind the bed, when a rather bedraggled Jeremy Hartley-Jones risked a quick look round the bedroom door. What he saw made him make a strategic retreat, as Andy set about ripping up Janice's expensive clothes one by one.

"He's going berserk. How long are they going to be, do you think?" Jeremy was whispering into his mobile, which had miraculously survived its dunking, and was in contact with the office. He had called in as soon as he realised what Andy was doing and had asked his father to phone the police, while he kept up a running commentary on the demolition work being carried out upstairs. "God knows why this madman has taken it into his head to attack this house, but it's bloody scary, Dad, I can tell you. I'm on my way downstairs now, before he decides to have a go at me."

In the distance, sirens could be heard and were getting closer. Jeremy rushed out of the front door and into the road, waving his arms wildly, as the police car turned into Castle Avenue.

Upstairs, Andy Davidson was really getting into his stride with the baseball bat and was working his way methodically through Janice's en-suite bathroom, which was beginning to look more like a building site every minute. He was unfazed by the imminent arrival of the police and, in fact, seemed to be smiling at the thought of being caught red-handed.

*

John Goodland roared off onto the Silverstone track, waving and leaving Crowther and Collins staring after his vanishing rear end.

"Never could understand it, you know," muttered Crowther.

"Understand what?" Collins asked, staring intently at the car as it was heading for the first bend.

"Motor racing, or rather the lure of it to be exact. Standing around in a light drizzle, watching a million pounds worth of car, flashing by at over 200 miles per hour, in a blur of adverts for Marlborough, isn't my idea of an afternoon out, I can tell you!"

"Oh, I don't know," she said, somewhat dreamily, as she watched Goodland negotiate the bend with skill.

"There he goes, Stirling Moss with a full head of hair. I'd love to do him for speeding, the cocky bastard, I really would."

"Mmmm."

"You fancy him, don't you?"

"What! Course I don't,' protested Collins and hurriedly headed for Crowther's car, "but I must admit there is something about speed and danger and that kind of arrogance that…"

"…that turns you on. Yes, I know, I know."

"No, it doesn't 'turn me on'! And you don't know what you're talking about…sir."

Was Collins protesting too much, thought Crowther? "All right. All right. Calm down. Anyway, I bet his house in Brighton will be a right mess."

They had reached Crowther's car and proceeded to get in.

"What do you mean 'His house will be a right mess'?"

"Well, I bet every time he opens a bottle of Champagne, he sprays it all over the living room walls for practice...just in case he ever wins. What a waste that is! Moet et Chandon must turn in their graves, the pair of 'em. Ready?"

He started the car and attempted a wheel-spin start, which unfortunately didn't quite work and resulted in a skid across the Pits, narrowly missing a group of mechanics who dived for cover.

*

Janice Holloway and Jason had just arrived home from the Leisure Centre Gym and were standing by the BMW, looking on in amazement, as Andy Davidson was bundled into the back of the police car and seated next to a uniformed PC. Andy didn't put up any resistance and seemed curiously at ease with the whole business. The other uniformed PC, who had been doing the 'bundling', got in the driving seat and reversed out of the drive.

Jason looked at Janice with a puzzled expression on his face. She shrugged her shoulders, as if to say 'Don't ask me. I've no idea either.'

As the car swung across the end of the drive, Andy could be seen through the rear side window. He smiled broadly, blew Janice a kiss and snuggled down for the ride.

She turned on her heel and stormed off towards the house, pursued by an anxious Jason.

*

In the CID room at Pemborough Police Station, Crowther had marked up a flip-sheet with the motorbike's locations and various train times. He was addressing the whole team and, throughout his briefing, pointed to the relevant facts.

"Quick recap, everybody," Crowther brought the meeting to order. "Have a look at this."

He revealed the flip-sheet and let the team take in its contents before launching into what he had to say.

MOTORBIKE (Known whereabouts)   **TRAIN TIMES**

THURSDAY 8th AUGUST

BRIGHTON: 6.45am (Owner parks bike)	**6.55am (Owner's train leaves)**	
7.00am (Stolen and ridden off)	**2.15pm (Goodlands' train leaves)**	

OXFORD: 10.07am (Pay and Display all day)	10.20am (North)	10.22am (South)

MURDER SCENE:
5.10pm (Jehovah's Witnesses see bike
leaving Sir Harold's house)

BANBURY: 5.20pm (Parking Attendant: time bike was parked)	5.22pm (North)	5.25pm (South)

FRIDAY 9th AUGUST
BANBURY: 9.30am & 3.30pm (Attendant sees bike and fixes penalty tickets)

NB: Bike still there on Monday. Reported to local police by Parking Attendant.

"Right. Listen up. The owner of the motorbike parks it at Brighton Railway Station at 6.45am last Thursday, in time for him to catch his usual 6.55am train. OK? Now:

Our alleged killer steals the bike (how, we're not sure, but he does) and has it away at around 7.00am.

The killer rides the bike to Oxford in around three hours. Forensic confirm that journey by uncovering an Oxford Railway Station car park pay-and-display ticket, timed at 10.07am and for all-day parking, suggesting that the bike may have been, and probably was, left there until...

3)...sometime that afternoon, when our Jehovah's Witnesses saw an identical bike, which we firmly believe to be the bike in question, leaving Sir Harold's house at about 5.10pm.

4) Ten minutes or so later, at around 5.25pm, in Banbury Railway Station car park, a parking attendant noticed the bike for the first time on his way home after work. He subsequently ticketed the bike at 9.30am and 3.30pm on the following day, Friday. When it was still there after the weekend, on Monday, he reported it to the local police.

Now, according to that parking attendant, the killer must have left the bike there after

5.15pm, when he finished work and locked up, but before 5.25pm, when he left to go home and he first saw it. Otherwise, if he'd seen it at 5.15pm, he would have checked its ticket. He didn't. Therefore, the bike was almost certainly left there at around 5.20pm.

Right. So, just after that time, there is the 5.22pm north to Birmingham and beyond, and the 5.25pm south to Oxford. Anybody seen buying a ticket at Banbury last Thursday around those times?"

"Yes, sir," said a young DC. "The woman on duty says a couple with a babe-in-arms bought tickets to Oxford to see their relatives, and two old age pensioners, with senior railcards, were off to the Fortune Theatre in London to see The Mousetrap, for the second time. They love it."

The whole team looked at the DC, puzzled by such impressive detail coming from one so young. The DC looked up from his pocket-book, saw he had attracted their attention and, it has to be said, made quite a meal of his explanation.

"In case you're wondering how I know all that, the ticket clerk lives next door to the couple with the baby, he's called Darren, by the way, the baby that is, 7lbs 6oz at birth. The OAPs, for your further information, were my Grandma and Grandad celebrating their Golden Wedding Anniversary. Other than a few more locals, of insignificant importance, there was no one else who bought a ticket. It's a small world is Banbury."

"Evidently," Crowther smiled to himself. "And we're grateful for the extent of your local knowledge. Thanks. What about after the 10.07am pay-and-display ticket at Oxford, Liz?"

"Yes, sir. The guy at Oxford remembers a man buying two tickets not long after 10.00am: a return ticket to Brighton and a single from Banbury to Birmingham. No great description, I'm afraid. He remembered him because he had a black crash helmet on, which he seemed unwilling to take off, was wearing a smart suit, and also, it seemed an odd pair of tickets to buy, since the man appeared to be on his own. I can see what he meant: a return to Brighton and a single from Banbury to Birmingham, both for that day. A bit odd."

"Yes, true. Although, if you factor in the bike, it might make some sense. I mean, with those tickets he could have gone south on the 10.22am, say, returned later to pick up the bike and get to Sir Harold's by 5.00pm, and then he could have got to Banbury in time for the 5.22pm to Birmingham. Don't ask me why he was going up and down the country like that, because I've no idea, but somewhere in the midst of all that there might just be a reason. Anybody got any ideas?"

Crowther looked appealingly at the team, without much luck.

They were all saved from any further embarrassment by a knock on the door and the appearance of Sergeant Trevor Beech. He apologised for the interruption and crossed to Crowther.

"Sorry, sir, but this has just come in. Thought you'd want to see it straightaway," said Beech, handing over a slim Report Folder.

"No problem," replied Crowther, as he quickly scanned the document. "Interesting. I'll be back, everybody, so see what you can make of it all," he said, as he left the room and went along the corridor towards his office, followed by Sergeant Beech. "Our Mr Graham Kirk, eh? That's more helpful than you know, Trevor. Thanks."

"That's not all, I'm afraid, sir. We've got a nutter in No.2. Says you're the only one who'll be able to understand him."

"I could take offence at that, Trevor, do you know that? What's he done?"

"Smashed up a house and pushed an Estate Agent into a swimming-pool."

'Can't be all that bad then. Isn't that everyone's ambition? You sort it out."

"More importantly, he wants to confess to a murder."

"Seriously?"

Crowther had stopped dead and turned to Beech.

"Seriously, sir."

*

In cell No.2, Andy Davidson was slumped on a chair, mumbling to himself and occasionally smiling at the thought of what he had managed to set up. As far as he was concerned it was all going to plan, and the coming interview with the DCI would clinch it. He looked up as Beech unlocked the door and opened it to let Crowther in.

"Hello, Mr. Crowther," said Andy, smiling and rising from his chair.

"Bloody Hell! Andy Davidson, as I live and breathe. Good grief. It's all right, Trevor, you can leave me alone with this one, I'll be fine. We're old friends, well, after a fashion." Beech left, and Crowther and Davidson, rather incongruously in the circumstances, shook hands. "Good to see you, I suppose. Have a seat. Thought you were inside. Don't tell me you've done a runner!"

"Just got out on parole."

"Didn't take you long to get back in again, did it? What's this all about?"

"Well, you know I got three years for the…erm...accident?"

"Oh, come off it. 'Causing death while pissed', I think is the legal term you're looking for. You should have got ten at least. Be honest."

"All right. You win some, OK? The point is - is it right that you can't be done for the same thing twice?"

"Depends what you mean by 'the same thing', I suppose. What's it to you?"

"It wasn't an accident, Mr. Crowther. It was murder. I did it deliberately."

"Bugger me! Do you know, I never realised that it was this week."

"What? What's this week?"

"National Confession Day. What the hell are you talking about, Andy?"

"The man I killed was Charlie Holloway."

"I know. I was there when they scraped him off your bumper."

"The house I smashed up just now belongs to his widow, Janice."

"There's no stopping you when somebody's upset you, is there?"

"The thing is, you see, Janice and me were together."

"Lucky Janice. So?"

"So...nobody knew, see? She wanted rid of Charlie, so we could get his money. He was loaded. She had this idea."

"Oh, I see. It was all her fault. Course it was."

"You're not making this easy."

"It's a job. OK, go on. She had this idea. What idea?"

"If I got myself all boozed up and ran him over, I'd only get a year or so with good behaviour. Might even get a suspended sentence. You read about it all the time these days - drunk drivers getting off light."

"And you fell for it?"

"I was mad for her, so I did it, yeh. And she was right. I only got three years. With good behaviour I was out on parole in half the time. Well, here I am to prove it. It was brilliant. It worked. A year and a half was no problem, with Janice and over a million quid waiting for me…only, it wasn't, and neither was she."

"Andy, old son, if you're looking for some sort of guarantee, you'd be better off at Curry's. We don't do them."

"Look, I don't care if I do go down again, Mr. Crowther, as long as that bitch goes down as well."

"Conspiracy to murder? Tricky one is that. Difficult to prove, you see. She'll just say you're doing it out of spite. Her word against yours."

"No, it isn't. I've got this." Andy said, as he reached into his trouser pocket and produced a worn piece of paper. He handed it to Crowther, who read it.

"Is this for real?"

"Oh, yes, it's real all right. Even got the date on it, see, and finger-prints, no doubt. Proof?"

"I've seen worse. I may be some time, so don't go away, will you?"

Crowther pocketed the paper and left. Andy smiled to himself and settled down to wait. He had all the time in the world.

*

Across town, DS Banks was sitting in his car, waiting patiently for the Company Accountant, Tom Marchbanks, to finish work and appear out of Moorhouse Engineering Limited's office building. Banks had made sure that he was parked where Graham Kirk, Managing Director, could see him from his office window. He wanted Kirk to witness what was to follow but was perhaps more interested to find out what Marchbanks had to say about Kirk's alibi of being seen in the car park at around five o'clock on the day of the murder. It had just passed that time, when Marchbanks emerged through the main doors.

"Tom Marchbanks?" Banks' voice rather boomed across the car park, as he got out of his car and approached him.

"Yes?" asked a curious Marchbanks.

"DS Banks, Pemborough CID. May I have a word?"

From his office window, Graham Kirk looked down and did indeed witness the meeting. He watched the two men deep in conversation. Marchbanks looked a little uneasy and, as he glanced nervously up at the building, he saw an even more uneasy and nervous-looking Kirk, staring down at him. Banks glanced up, too, and was pleased to find that what he saw underlined his theory.

*

Maybe it was the schoolboy in him, but Crowther still got a thrill from driving a marked Police Panda Car at speed, with all systems flashing and blaring, and making the world and his wife get the hell out of the way. OK, it wasn't Formula 1 standard, but at least he could cope with speeding through a chicane of queuing traffic and screaming safely over a pedestrian crossing, which was more than John 'fancy pants' Goodland had to face on his sanitised circuit. With that somewhat childish thought in mind and with butterflies in his stomach, Crowther, accompanied by a uniformed WPC, flew along Castle Avenue and screeched to a halt outside the Holloway residence. They both got out, the WPC somewhat relieved at having survived the trip at all, and went to the front door. Crowther rang the bell and waited patiently.

After a minute or so, Jason answered the door, but before he had chance to open his mouth, Crowther flashed his ID and went straight in.

"DCI Crowther, WPC Reynolds, Pemborough CID. And you are?"

"Jason…"

"Hello, Jason. Where's Janice Holloway?"

"Through there, straight ahead. Look, is this about that idiot who trashed the place? 'Cos if it is…"

"Yes, it is, actually. Through the Conservatory?"

Jason was almost running to keep up with them, as they crossed the lounge, exited via the Conservatory and emerged onto the patio. Janice, wearing her favourite bikini, was sunning herself by the pool. She had heard most of the conversation, so she knew what was coming, or thought she did, and lay on her sun lounger, relaxed and sipping a drink.

"Mrs. Janice Holloway?" asked Crowther, politely.

"Yes. I take it you've got that maniac, Andy Davidson, locked up by now. The mess he made of this place! It's unbelievable!?"

"You won't be seeing him again, I can assure you."

"Good riddance."

"But then, you won't be seeing anybody for a while, will you?"

"Nope. I'm moving to Spain."

"A little closer to home, I think, Mrs Holloway. Do you mind if we discuss your travel arrangements down at the station?"

"You what? What for?"

"Just something Andy Davidson said, in passing."

"What's that lying little toe-rag been saying now? He killed my husband, isn't that enough?"

"Not quite. He says that was all your idea."

"And you believe him? Gordon Bennet! Even a copper can't be that thick. Show these plods out, Jason, for God's sake."

"No, I didn't believe him…until he showed me this," Crowther announced, as he produced the piece of paper Andy had given him. "It's the note that you left under his windscreen wiper. He'd kept it and only found it again when he came out of nick and got all his gear back. It had been packed up with the clothes he left with a mate for well over a year, but it's in remarkably good condition, considering. We've lifted several different sets of fingerprints from it, of course, and yours came out rather well. Even if they hadn't, it wouldn't be difficult to prove it's in your handwriting and, funnily enough, it's dated the day of your husband's untimely death. It does go on a bit, I must say, but this is the bit I like, though:

'Remember, Andy, don't be late, 'cos I've made sure Charlie will be walking down Beechwood Road tonight between 7.00pm and 7.30pm on his way to the club, and he'll be alone. Drink enough scotch, or whatever you want, to make sure your well over the limit, and take the bastard out. You've got to make sure you finish him off, 'cos with him dead, my darling, we'll have the rest of our lives together to spend his bloody money. It'll work, believe me. I love you. Janice, The Merry Widow!'

Oh, I do like that, I really do - 'The Merry Widow' - what a lovely touch. Nice one, Janice. By the way, there's a car waiting for you outside. WPC Reynolds here will help you get dressed, while she reads you your rights. Amazing coincidence, isn't it, Janice, your surname being the same as the prison - Holloway?"

CHAPTER SEVEN

Wednesday, August 14th, 1991: 8.30am

If he were honest, DS David Banks looked and felt like a schoolboy reporting to the Headmaster.

He was standing, almost to attention, by the side of Detective Chief Superintendent Vance, who was seated at his desk, resplendent in full uniform and reading through a report folder. Banks rarely had the chance to disturb the sanctity of the DCS's office and was glad of the opportunity to lay his theory in person before Vance, thus leapfrogging Crowther in the station hierarchy, while the latter wasn't around.

"Would you ask DCI Crowther if he could pop along to my office, if he wouldn't mind. Thank you," intoned Vance and put the phone down. "Well, you've certainly been busy, Banks. Anything else?"

"Yes, sir. There's his full statement," said Banks, placing it carefully before the DCS. "Says it all, I think, sir."

Vance picked up the statement form and started to read, nodding the while.

"Absolutely. Yes. Yes. Well done, Banks."

"Thank you, sir."

"Well done, indeed. So, it would appear that the mystery motorbike was a red herring."

"A red Suzuki, actually, sir," Banks said, keeping a straight face.

"Oh, absolutely. Where would we be without the Japanese, eh?"

"Where, indeed, as they say."

Before Banks had time to work out who was winding who up in these exchanges, there was a knock at the door and DCI Crowther came straight in.

"Ah, Colin. Morning. Thanks for popping in. DS Banks here has got us a suspect..."

"Graham Kirk," Crowther tossed the name in, as if it were insignificant.

"Splendid. Both working along the same lines, eh?"

"Oh, yes, sir. I've always admired DS Banks's unswerving allegiance to the bleeding obvious."

Crowther ignored Banks's stare while, true to form, Vance ignored Crowther's comment, appearing to be totally unmoved by the increasingly tense atmosphere, and carried on regardless, "A team working together. Just what we need, you know."

"If I may be allowed to say so, sir, you might recall that I am Chief Investigating Officer on this case, and it's a motive that is 'just what we need'."

"Absolutely, and we have got one, thanks to DS Banks's initiative. Spell it out again, would you, Banks, for Colin's benefit?"

"Yes, sir. Well...Colin," he began, dodging Crowther's glare, "Graham Kirk and Sir Harold Moorhouse didn't exactly get on, to say the least. It was Kirk who had increased his own shareholding a few years ago and forced Sir Harold to resign. Basically, he put the boot in and had him voted out. A rather nasty and ambitious piece of work is Kirk. You see, it transpires that they just didn't agree on which direction the company should be going. Sir Harold saw no reason to tamper with something that had been successful for nearly fifty years. Kirk, on the other hand, saw himself as the great innovator, who could transform an ageing business into a vehicle fit to take on the challenges of a changing engineering world, a world with which Sir Harold had completely lost touch, in Kirk's view.

However, Kirk had underestimated the wily old bird that he had ousted. Sir Harold had bided his time and was waiting for the right moment to repay Kirk's treachery by getting the rest of the Board, who had regretted his departure to a man, to pool their shareholding and elbow Kirk in revenge. That moment had come. Kirk would have lost £120,000 a year in salary and £100,000 in bonuses and share options."

"And just where did you uncover that little gem?" asked Crowther, grimly.

"Courtesy of Tom Marchbanks, the Company's Accountant, if you must know. He was leaving Kirk's office when I was there last Friday, and he looked none too happy, believe me. When I went back to interview Kirk again yesterday, I waited around and had a word with Marchbanks as he was leaving. He told me that he didn't go much on Kirk. Nobody did, apparently. Most of the staff hated his guts. Yes, Marchbanks was obviously in an extremely talkative mood, so I let him get it all off his chest. He told me that Kirk had asked him to be his alibi for around five o'clock on Thursday, by saying that he'd seen Kirk in the car park on that day, at that time - the day and the time of Sir Harold's murder."

"Did he really? Well, I never!"

"Oh, come on, Colin, give the man credit. See the bigger picture. We have everything now:

Evidence that Kirk was there: the prints on those papers.

Opportunity to do it: he was in the vicinity, and was vague about his movements, and now,

Motive to get rid of Sir Harold: he stood to lose the best part of a quarter of a million pounds."

"If you don't mind the technical jargon, sir, that's what we at the sharp end would call…a load of bollocks."

As if nothing at all untoward had happened, Vance said, "On the other hand, Colin, I'm sure you must agree that Detective Sergeant Banks has enough to bring Kirk in on suspicion."

"Sir, Detective Sergeant Banks has bugger all. The only things he has are:

A second-hand motive, based on hearsay from Marchbanks, a self-confessed, prejudiced pen-pusher.

An opportunity that wouldn't stand up in a light sodding breeze.

And fingerprint evidence that a pre-pubescent Barrister wouldn't wipe his arse with.

Yes, Kirk briefly popped into the frame. He quickly popped out again, when I received a report from Traffic, while DS Banks here was exercising his initiative, confirming Kirk's BMW as the car involved in a hit-and-run on a cyclist at 5.10pm last Thursday. Funnily enough, almost exactly the same time as Sir Harold Moorhouse was having his head caved in over thirty-five miles away. The cyclist is in Intensive Care, by the way, and has an evens chance of survival. That's why Kirk was 'twitchy', DS Banks. Did you manage to get all that? Good morning."

Crowther stormed out of the office. Vance closed the report folder and handed it back to Banks, who took it, exited sharpish and set off along the corridor after Crowther.

"Sir! Sir!"

"Second on the right."

"Sir?"

"My office, Banks, since you've obviously forgotten where it is."

As Crowther entered his office and sat at his desk, Banks caught up with him, still brandishing the discredited report and tried to crawl out of the massive hole he had dug for himself.

"OK, I was wrong, sir. But how was I to know that he'd been in a hit-and-run? There was evidence: his fingerprints, not conclusive, but enough..."

"Do you go to Night School for it?"

"For what?"

"Missing the bleeding point. Yes, there was evidence, after a fashion. Yes, he was a possible. But you come to me. You do not leapfrog to some Public School Mummy's Boy in a Fancy Dress!"

"But you weren't around, sir, and he is the boss, after all."

"In theory, yes, but in reality Vance is just a politician. His job is to make sure we can do our job, and that is all. He wouldn't know a fingerprint from a map of East Anglia."

Banks snorted in laughter and tried to cover it up by coughing.

"You repeat that, David, and I'll chew your balls off. Now, get out of my office and look both ways before you cross the road in future."

"Sir."

Banks retreated with as much dignity as he could muster, leaving Crowther still at his desk and looking rather pensive. He picked up the internal phone and dialled. There was obviously an almost immediate response.

"Liz?"

*

"God, I need this," said Crowther, taking a good drink of his pint. He was in the saloon bar of The Roebuck, where he had asked DC Liz Collins to join him.

"Where is he now?" she asked.

"Licking his wounds, I shouldn't wonder."

"Banks is alright…really," ignoring Crowther's knowing look, she carried on. "Oh, come on, you know he is, deep down. In any case, I'd have thought you of all people would have been mature enough not to take it out on him just because he got there before you."

"I need a pint, not counselling."

"I got the impression that what you need is to talk about it. But all right, I'll keep my mouth shut in future."

"Pack it in, Liz," said Crowther, taking a long swig of his drink. "You're right, though, damn your eyes. I'd have gone for Kirk in the same circumstances."

"You rotten bastard…sir."

"Well, Banks should know better than to go to the 'Almighty'. You've only got to mention the word 'suspect' to Vance, and he's off getting his uniform dry-cleaned for the Press Conference."

Crowther's mobile, which he had on the bar, rang out. He picked it up.

"Crowther. Hi…no, I'm in the office…oh, yes, when?...Ok, tell Ian that Friday's favourite for me, will you…ta…and you. See you later. Bye…"

As he put the phone back on the bar, he gave Collins an apologetic shrug.

"…I said I wouldn't come in the pub. I'm supposed to be cutting down. You know how it is."

"You don't have to explain to me. I'm not your wife."

"No, but you've got that same look on your face. How do women do that?"

"We don't. It's just that guilty men can always see it."

"Why should I feel guilty?"

"Only you know that."

"Not about Banks, anyway. He deserved it."

"About what, then?"

Crowther looked at her, and slowly nodded his head.

"You're your father's daughter, and that's a fact…"

He knew Collins had inherited her father's perceptive mind, and that she had instinctively clocked that Crowther had just admitted to harbouring some form of guilt.

"…if you must know, Liz…"

"I don't need to know…"

"…if you must know," he emphasised, "we've been trying for a baby for over a year."

"Ah, I see," she said, knowingly.

"What do you see?"

"The more you fail, the more you want it."

"Not necessarily."

"Is that a confession that I've just heard…?"

Collins watched him drink and furrowed her brow in thought.

"Of course not," Crowther answered her a tad too quick for belief.

"…because if it is, it's not fair on Allyson. You do realise that, don't you?"

"Yes, yes…hang about. You know what I just did on the phone?"

"Yes. You said you were at the office. You lied to your wife."

"Yes, I did. Easy, wasn't it? And she believed me."

"Why wouldn't she?"

"Exactly."

Crowther downed his pint, grabbed his phone and headed for the door, calling to Collins, "Come on. There's somebody we need to talk to."

*

As they drove out of Pemboough, Crowther explained to Collins the bare bones of what he had been thinking and how it fitted in with a theory he was slowly developing. While not exactly sharing his enthusiasm for the idea, she nevertheless indulged him and promised to go along with the line of questioning he wanted to pursue.

They pulled into the drive of Sir Harold's house, parked and were just approaching the front door, when it opened to reveal Anna Goodland dressed to go out.

"Oh, hello," said Anna. "It's you lot again, is it? Look, I'm just on my way into Oxford, shopping, and I'm afraid my husband isn't here. He's speed-testing the new car. Sorry to disappoint you." She was about to close the door, when Crowther stepped forward.

"No problem. It's you we wanted to talk to, anyway, and we won't keep you long. Could we have a brief word inside? Thank you."

He didn't wait for a response, and entered the house, followed by Collins.

"Well, really!" Anna had no choice but to trail along behind them, down the hallway and into the lounge. "I won't offer you a drink, as you won't be staying. So, what is it you want to know?"

"It's only a formality," said Crowther. "Nothing to worry about."

"We just need to fill in a few gaps, you see," Collins took up the questioning. "Could you clarify exactly what you and your husband did last Thursday?"

"What, everything?"

"If it's not too much trouble," Crowther's hint of sarcasm prompted Collins to try and calm things down.

"We really would appreciate it, Mrs Goodland."

"Very well, if I must go over it all again. We got up early…5/5.15am. John left for the office at 6.30am. I spent the morning packing for Manchester and tidying up."

"Any visitors? Phone calls, perhaps?"

"No. Not even the milkman. John had cancelled it. He thinks of everything. Oh, I phoned Mary Fellows, a friend, to tell her we'd be back by Monday evening, and I'd just put the phone down when John called to say he'd be working on and not to bother him."

"So, he specifically said that you were not to phone him?" asked Crowther.

"Correct. He said he would be in the Design Office and not to disturb him on any account. Not that I would. He often got engrossed in some technical stuff. Nothing unusual about it. Is that all?"

"What time was this?"

"9.30am, thereabouts."

"That's very helpful. Thank you."

"My pleasure, I'm sure. Now, if you'll excuse me," Anna said, gathering her handbag and car keys, and heading for the hallway. However, before she got to the door, Collins chipped in.

"You got to Manchester early evening, we understand."

"No idea. I suppose we must have. John would know."

"Doesn't matter," said Crowther. "Did you eat on the train?"

"Not as such. No dining car these days. John went for some coffee and sandwiches. Are our eating habits relevant to your enquiry?"

"Not crucial, no, but we like to fill in all the gaps. So, just for the record, what time did your husband go for the food?"

"I haven't the foggiest idea. Just before Oxford, at a guess. Yes, he said he wanted to speak to father, as well, so he took my phone. John won't have one. Hates them. He took his briefcase and some papers to do with the gears or some such thing and came back with the food, such as it was."

"Must have taken him quite a while, phoning, queueing for food, carrying coffee, sandwiches and his briefcase."

"I suppose it must. I don't really know. I dozed off for a while, half an hour or more, but we were past Banbury, I know that. I half heard the Guard's announcement. Look, is that all? I have got a life to lead, you know."

"Yes, that's all. Sorry we had to disturb your life over something as mundane as the search for whoever ended your father's. Good afternoon."

Even Collins was shocked by Crowther's cutting remark, as they left the house, got in the car and sped away towards Pemborough.

*

"John Goodland? You're joking. What are you suggesting he did? Got off the Manchester train at Oxford, hopped on a motorbike, that had magically got there from Brighton, drove to Sir Harold's, killed him and then carried on to Banbury in time to catch the train that he'd just got off?"

Crowther was by no means 100% sure, as he tried to make his answer to Banks's question sound feasible. The rest of the team, gathered in the CID office and, equally sceptical, waited for his reply.

"Well, in a word...yes. That's what I'm suggesting."

"Oh, get real...sir!"

"Hear me out, everybody. Look, I know it's pushing credibility a bit..."

"A bit? Give it a rest!"

"...but it explains a hell of a lot. Bear with me. Now, you've all seen this before." Crowther turned over the flip sheet with the motorbike's whereabouts, train times and the general timescale of events.

MOTORBIKE (Known whereabouts)			TRAIN TIMES

THURSDAY 8th AUGUST

BRIGHTON:	6.45am (Owner parks bike)		6.55am (Owner's train leaves)
	7.00am (Stolen and ridden off)		2.15pm (Goodlands' train leaves)

OXFORD:	10.07am (Pay and Display all day)	10.20am (North)	10.22am (South)

MURDER SCENE:
5.10pm (Jehovah's Witnesses see bike
leaving Sir Harold's house)

BANBURY:	5.20pm (Parking Attendant: time bike was parked)	5.22pm (North)	5.25pm (South)

FRIDAY 9th AUGUST
BANBURY: 9.30am & 3.30pm (Attendant sees bike and fixes penalty tickets)

NB: Bike still there on Monday. Reported to local police by Parking Attendant.

"It explains why the bike was stolen in Brighton and left at Oxford. It didn't get there 'magically' at all. It got there because Goodland was in Brighton and needed a fast bike in Oxford to get to Sir Harold's and then on to Banbury as fast as he could..."

"But, sir, he didn't get to Sir Harold's until after five o'clock, when the Jehovah's Witnesses saw him. So, where was he all that time...?" interrupted Collins, but Crowther ploughed on.

"...and it explains that very seven hour gap until 5.10pm. After he'd stolen the bike in Brighton and ridden it to Oxford, obviously he had to go back on a train to pick up his wife, so they could both catch the 2.15pm to Manchester. A train, by the way, that passes between Oxford and Banbury, during which time his wife admits he wasn't with her.

It also explains the two train tickets that he bought at Oxford Railway Station after he had parked the bike there. The return ticket was so he could go straight back to Brighton, then later on to get off the 2.15pm Brighton to Manchester train at Oxford and pick up the bike. The single ticket from Banbury, remember it? was needed to let him get straight onto the platform at Banbury quickly, so he could rejoin that Manchester train going north. Plus, it explains why he made the journey from the murder scene to Banbury in such a hurry - because he had to catch that train."

Banks, who had been listening carefully, seemed determined to pick holes in what he thought was an unbelievably dodgy theory, "Sorry, but what it doesn't explain is the fact that he was in Brighton at 9.30am! His wife spoke to him at the office. According to your 'theory' he must have been tearing round the M25 at 9.30am! But he couldn't have been, because he was in his office!"

Collins joined in, "And it doesn't explain the content of the answering machine messages. He was on the train leaving Oxford when he made the first call. He phoned half an hour later at 5.23pm, after the train had left Banbury. The times fit perfectly. We've been through all this before."

"Absolutely. Good grief, he's got me at it now! Listen, all you're doing is repeating what Goodland said."

"No, we're not," Banks insisted. "His wife told us he was in his office at 9.30am."

"Because he *said* he was. He phoned her, remember? She believed him. Wives do," replied Crowther, with a sheepish look to Collins. "She told us he said he was phoning from his office at 9.30am, and not to call him back. She believed him and we believed her; why shouldn't we? Neither of them were under suspicion at the time, but Goodland could have been anywhere at 9.30am, couldn't he?"

"Yeees…I suppose so. But what about the answering machine?"

"Same thing. He *said* the train was leaving Oxford. He *said* he'd call again in half an hour, and in that call he *said* they were nearing Banbury. Now, we know that second call was made at 5.23pm, so he was definitely on the train, and it had just left Banbury, but the first call could have been made only a minute earlier, say, at 5.22pm, when he wasn't on the train leaving Oxford, but on the train leaving Banbury."

"With respect, sir..."

"Cut the crap, Banks, say what you think."

"I think you've got yourself some wild theory and you're squeezing everything in to fit it. 'Sod the facts, lads, let's make it work.' Well, here's a fact for you: Oxford to Banbury via the murder scene must be nearly thirty miles. If your wild theory's correct, he must have done it in…what? just over twenty minutes, including the murder. Impossible!"

"There's only one way to find out, isn't there?"

Banks, Collins and the rest of the team looked at each other, wondering what Crowther had in mind. They would find out soon enough.

*

At going on for five o'clock later that day, and just before Oxford's rush hour could get into full swing, Banks, Collins and a uniformed driver found themselves waiting in a marked car at the exit to Oxford Railway Station car park. Crowther was on Platform 2 ready for the arrival of the train to Manchester, which was on its through journey from Brighton. As soon as it came to a halt, he would run along the platform, cross through the barrier, join the others in the car and they would set off, at speed, towards Banbury, via Sir Harold's house. Crowther's plan depended not so much on the reliability of that particular train, but rather on what could be achieved between its arrival at Oxford (estimated at 4.57pm and due out at 4.59pm) and its subsequent departure from Banbury (timed at 5.22pm), an absolute maximum of twenty-five minutes. He was up against it, and he knew it. Either he was about to prove his outrageous theory absolutely correct, or he was about to look an absolutely prize plonker.

4.56.30sec: The Manchester train drew into Oxford station, as the loudspeaker was announcing, '...now arriving at Platform 2 is the 16.59 to Manchester Piccadilly, calling at Banbury, Birmingham International, Birmingham New Street...'

Crowther waited for it to come to a complete halt and for the doors to open. He then ran for the exit barrier, showed his ID to the ticket collector, who had been pre-warned, and headed for the car park, where the marked car was waiting. He got into the front passenger seat, and as the driver was about to speed off, Crowther held up his hand to stop him.

"Hold it," he ordered. "Let's think about what our murderer must have had to do before he left, and how long it must've taken him. Now, he's using the motorbike, remember. So, he takes the black crash helmet out of his shoulder bag and puts it on, straps the bag to the pillion and starts up the bike: how, I don't know, but he was in the trade so it's not unreasonable to assume he knew what to do, or he had got hold of a set of keys somehow. Right, let's say it takes him…this long to do all that." Crowther looked carefully at his watch, paused for a couple more seconds and said, "OK, let's go!"

4.58.15sec: THE PATROL CAR SCREECHED OFF, SIREN BLARING.
THE TRAIN WAS ABOUT TO LEAVE THE STATION, AS
THE PATROL CAR EXITED THE CAR PARK ONTO THE
A420 WEST OUT OF OXFORD, THEN NORTH ON TO
5.00.30sec: THE A34 AT THE BOTLEY ROUNDABOUT.
AFTER 10 MILES ON DUAL CARRIAGEWAY,
5.06.30sec: THE CAR JOINED THE NEWLY OPENED M40 AT
JUNCTION 9, COVERED THE 5 MILES TO JUNCTION 10
AT OVER 120MPH,
5.09.00sec: AND TURNED OFF TO ARDLEY.
SIR HAROLD'S HOUSE WAS 350YDS DOWN THE
ROAD TO FRITWELL.
5.09.10sec: THE PATROL CAR PULLED UP OUTSIDE.

"Just over twelve minutes from getting off the train," announced Crowther.

"Yes, but he wouldn't have had a siren going hell for leather, would he?" Banks pointed out, somewhat unnecessarily.

"No, we know that, but he was on a bike that could outmanoeuvre and outrun this clapped out old thing. No offence, driver. And don't forget, Goodland's not exactly a stranger to speed, is he?"

"That's another thing. What if he'd got caught?"

"Then he couldn't have committed the murder, could he? And we wouldn't be sitting here listening to you wittering on, would we? There was bound to be a risk, but he no doubt reckoned he could drive his way out of any situation, especially now on mostly Motorway, and he was probably right. Now shut up. OK?"

Crowther checked his watch again.

"Now, how long do we reckon he was here at Sir Harold's? Let's see - he parks the bike, unhooks the bag, goes into the house, down the hallway and into the study. He takes out a weapon (maybe cutters he must've used on the bike), belts Sir Harold three times and puts it back in his bag. He leaves papers with Kirk's prints on, to throw us off the scent, makes sure the answering machine is on and goes back to the bike! How long?"

"Not long. For what it's worth, a couple of minutes, maybe, if he ran," offered Collins.

"With the pressure he was under I'd say he probably ran like hell, and it could've been as low as ninety seconds. But OK, let's go the other way. Let's call it nearer to three minutes, which is about...now. Off we go."

5.11.50sec: THE CAR CAREERED OFF DOWN THE LANE, REJOINED THE
               M40 AND WENT NORTH TOWARDS JUNCTION 11, WHERE IT
5.17.55sec: LEFT THE M40 AND HEADED FOR BANBURY TOWN CENTRE,
5.19.07sec: TURNED INTO THE ROAD TO BANBURY RAILWAY STATION AND
5.19.56sec: CAME TO A HALT IN BANBURY RAILWAY STATION CAR PARK.

"26.7 miles, all told, in just under 23 minutes," said Crowther, checking the time and the car's trip mileage. "So, what did he have to do then? Well, he must have taken off the helmet, put it in the bag, got out his pre-bought train ticket to pass through the barrier and strolled onto the platform. Come on, then, what are we waiting for? Let's do it."

Crowther walked quite slowly to the ticket barrier. He was followed by Banks and Collins, both looking decidedly uncertain about what their reaction was going to be to Crowther's unfolding plan. They each showed their ID to the ticket collector and walked onto the platform.

5.20.47sec: The Brighton to Manchester train had just come to a halt, and the station announcer was saying, 'The train now standing at Platform 1 is the 17.22 for Manchester Piccadilly, calling at Birmingham International, Birmingham New Street...'

A justifiably smug Crowther opened a carriage door to let passengers off and turned to his team, "Now tell me it's impossible!"

193

"OK. OK. Agreed, it is possible," Banks admitted, holding up his hands in submission. "But where's the proof?'"

"Fucked if I know. Got any ideas?"

CHAPTER EIGHT

Thursday, August 15th, 1991: 8.05am

"Why does he want all this, Sarg?"

"Don't ask, lad. He's like a dog with a bone when he gets going."

PC Peter Parker and Sergeant Trevor Beech were struggling with a mass of files, statements, motorbike specifications, answering machine tapes etc. etc. on their way to Crowther's office. They had been told to gather up all documents relevant to Sir Harold Moorhouse's murder, and to put them in chronological order for further detailed examination.

"But what's he going to do with it all? We know what's here already."

"Listen, somewhere in the middle of this lot might just be the tiny piece of evidence that's missing. If it's there, he'll find it. If it isn't, and he doesn't, you can kiss goodbye to that week's leave you've been looking forward to."

"Bit Sherlock Holmes, isn't it? Or, to put it bluntly, arrogant."

"Steady. You might think that, lad, and I have to admit that's what I used to think, but after years of indulging him, I have to grudgingly admit that...well, it works. Give him time and there's a fair chance he'll come up with the solution."

Beech knocked on the office door and entered on Crowther's call.

"Come in. Ah, Trevor. Thanks," said Crowther, while busy writing tags for Allyson's birthday presents. His desk and chair were covered in bags, paper, wrapped presents and items yet to be tagged.

"On the desk, sir?"

"Yes...ah, no, better not. On the floor. I'll sort it all out. Cheers."

"Sir."

Beech and Parker laid all they were carrying under the window and left.

*

Later that day, the CID office was packed in anticipation of Crowther's midday briefing that he had hurriedly called only an hour or so earlier.

DS Banks, DC Collins and the whole of the rest of the team were there, all wondering what was so important that they had been summoned at such short notice from their various tasks. PC Parker, standing by the door next to Sergeant Beech, felt himself privileged to have been invited, ordered really, to attend a CID briefing. Police Constable Peter 'four-star' Parker had been on the Pemborough force for less than a year. His had been a remarkably undistinguished start to a career that he had hoped would take him fast-track into CID. It didn't. However, what he lacked in fundamental suitability for the job, he more than made up for in enthusiasm, misguided as it often turned out to be.

His nickname, 'four-star', derived from an incident in his third month with Traffic, when his endearing keenness caused him to forget to check the amount of petrol in the Panda car, and he ran out of juice on the A38, while chasing a stolen Ford Transit. The AA patrol man, whom P.C. Parker had flagged down, was sympathetic, if somewhat amused, and kindly towed him back to Pemborough Police HQ. Unfortunately for Parker, they arrived just in time to run the gauntlet of a complete shift change. The slow handclap from his colleagues, as he was towed into the car park, did nothing to improve his mood. He was taken off the cars, put back on the beat and 'four-star' was born.

If truth be told, Parker was only present in the CID office because Crowther had the feeling he was going to need all the manpower he could get to prove that Goodland had actually done what Crowther had clearly demonstrated he could have done.

"I thought he said twelve o'clock. It's twenty-past already. Is he always as late as this?" Parker chirped up to Sergeant Beech.

"I've told you, he's a law unto himself. You'll find out."

A young Detective Sergeant came rushing in, expecting the briefing to be in full swing.

"Sorry I'm late, sir…oh, where is he?"

"Closeted in his office, doing his Benedictine monk impersonation," said Banks, indicating Crowther's door, which at that very moment had opened.

"Trappist, to be strictly correct. You should try it. Sorry to keep you everybody. Now, listen up. We progress. Slowly, but we progress. Right. I want us to consider John Goodland, Sir Harold Moorhouse's charming son-in-law. So…

Motive: his wife's inheritance.

Opportunity: well, he did have it, assuming my train theory isn't too ridiculously tight for time.

Evidence: bloody nuisance, I know, but the Courts will insist on it. So, here we go. Goodland doesn't have a mobile phone. However, the land line telephone company has confirmed that the only call made from his office last Thursday was at 1.29pm for a taxi to pick up his charming wife.

So, he didn't call her from there at 9.30am, like he said he did. That means all you lot have to do is find out which of the remaining thirty-odd million phones he did call her from."

There was a knock at the door, a PC entered and passed a report form to Sergeant Beech, who briefly scanned it and held it up for Crowther to see.

"What is it, Trevor?"

"Just come through from Banbury, sir, as far as I can tell. Marked 'urgent' for your attention." Beech passed the form to Crowther.

"Ta," he said, and quickly read through it. "Surprise, surprise. We really do progress. Guess what's just turned up? A black crash helmet and a pair of blood-stained metal cutters. Bet you Lost Property haven't had them reported missing."

"Where was this?" asked Collins.

"Three miles north of Banbury, in a farmer's field. Where? Next to the railway line."

Emboldened by his new role as a PC attached to the CID department, Parker felt moved to chip in with his own thoughts on the matter. "I reckon Goodland threw them out of the window, sir."

"You're after my job, aren't you, four-star?" There was some sympathetic laughter. "No, no, fair enough, it's a good point and he's probably right. Thank you, Parker. Now, Forensics say that it's definitely Sir Harold's blood group, but apart from that and Goodland's circumstantial involvement, there's only smudged prints, traces of wheat and what appears to be rabbit pooh."

There was no stopping Parker by this time. He just couldn't stop himself from saying, "Shall I bring him in, sir?"

"Who, the rabbit?" chimed in Banks, to much snorting and laughing from the team.

"Not yet, but you could always put a tail on him!" said Crowther, smiling, accompanied by even greater laughter all round. "All right, folks, that'll do. No, Parker, thanks, we just haven't got enough yet. Tell you who you can bring in, though - a sound engineer and the owner of the bike."

The team had mostly quietened down, but started to mutter amongst themselves, wondering what Crowther had spotted now.

*

PC Parker was laden down with wrapped gifts for Allyson Crowther's birthday, as he stumbled out of the rear exit of Pemborough HQ and into the car park. Crowther had opened the boot of his car, had carefully laid a bouquet of flowers next to a bottle of champagne and proceeded to take the gifts of trousers, perfume, underwear etc. off Parker.

"You married, four-sta...Parker?"

"Thinking about it, sir."

"Really? A word to the wise: pick somebody whose birthday is either the 14th February or the 25th December. That way, once a year you can kill two birds with one stone and save yourself a whole lot of trouble, not to mention money."

"Yes, sir."

Crowther put the last package into the boot and closed it.

"Thanks for that. I'll be back at two o'clock. If either the sound engineer or the bike owner turns up, I'll be in the pub, on my mobile."

He headed out of the car park, leaving Parker to wander back into the station, desperately trying to recall if his girlfriend's birthday was possibly in either February or December.

*

The Saloon Bar of The Roebuck was never all that busy on a Thursday lunchtime, and so it proved to be on that particular day. In fact, Ian Harper, Crowther's electrician friend, was the only customer and was perched on a bar stool staring at two half-finished pints of bitter and an open packet of cheese and onion crisps.

Two girls in tight jeans giggled as they came out of the Ladies, walked past and prompted Harper to turn and stare at their denim-clad rear ends. At the same moment, Crowther emerged from the Gents, crossed to the bar and joined Harper in his intense examination.

"If you're thinking what I'm thinking, you're under arrest," said Crowther.

The girls vanished into the Lounge Bar and, with the show over, the two spectators concentrated on their unfinished pints.

"You know what they say, don't you?" said Harper. "Men think about sex every six seconds."

"They should be so lucky. I have to think about it all the bloody time!"

"Ah. No joy on the baby front, I take it."

"Not a sausage."

"No comment. Maybe you're firing blanks. Ever thought of that, have you?"

"Thank you, Ian. That is so helpful. Thanks a lot."

"I'm only saying. Anyway, you don't want to be bothered with all that 'happy families' stuff at your time of life, and I know, mate. I'll tell you something about having kids - after we had finished having ours, I got my first full night's sleep about the time our youngest passed through puberty. And you can kiss goodbye to your social life, I can tell you."

"Your mission in life, isn't it? Cheering me up."

"Forewarned is forearmed, Colin. That's all I'm saying."

"Mmm, I know. To tell you the truth, it's getting a bit much already - what with the pair of us on edge all the time."

"Allyson been giving you earache about it, has she?"

"And some. She said I never listen to what she says - at least I think that's what she said."

"I know the feeling. So, having second thoughts, are we?"

"Feeling guilty, more like."

"Oh, yes. What have you been up to?"

"Huh! Chance would be a fine thing. No, it's just that I've been rushing around all week sorting out her birthday presents, when I know damn well that the only thing she really wants is the one thing I can't give her."

"Can't or won't?"

"If I can't, Ian, then the 'won't' is academic, isn't it?'

They both went back to leaning on the bar and lost themselves in their pints, mulling over the whole situation, until Harper broke the spell.

"Fancy a game at the weekend?" he said and brought them both back to reality.

"Sod it. Why not. Life must go on after all, and with a bit of luck I'll have this latest case under wraps by tomorrow."

"That'll be the Moorhouse murder, will it?"

"Yes. Might well be a good result. If it's all done and dusted within the week, I'll be looking at a personal best. Fantastic."

"Good for you. I read about it, of course. Is it right that he had his head completely smashed in?"

"Certainly is. Brains all over the Axminster. Have a crisp."

"Oh, ta. Go on then, tell us. Who did it?"

"I can't tell you that. Anyway, I don't know for sure, do I?' Looking round to make certain they were still on their own, Crowther whispered, "Listen. You won't say a word?"

"Of course not. You know me."

"That's the problem."

"Give over. You know damn well I won't say anything."

"Not even to your wife?"

"Not to anybody's wife."

"Promise?"

"Oh, for God's sake! Yes, I promise. So, who did it?"

"I hope I don't regret this. Sir Harold Moorhouse was found in his Study; Forensics say he was killed with a long piece of metal; the killer was a Professor Plum."

"Piss off!"

"Watch the news tomorrow, then. See Vance taking all the credit; what there is of it."

"Is he the bloke who got the job that you were after?"

"I wasn't all that bothered, as it happens. Didn't fancy playing politics anyway." Crowther finished his pint and eased himself off the bar stool, saying, "Look, Allyson will be coming out of work any sec. I better go and meet her. Back in a minute, with any luck."

"Don't bother. I'll walk over with you. I'm working at her Bank, as it happens."

"Oh, right."

Crowther opened the door and they both emerged onto Pemborough High Street, which was busy with lunchtime traffic and pedestrians.

"I'll book a court for midday Saturday, shall I?" Crowther offered.

"Make it a bit later, say, one o'clock. I've got to drop my sister and her kids off at the Wacky Warehouse around midday."

"The Wacky what?"

"Don't ask."

"I just did, but I get the feeling I don't really want to know. Oh, by the way, tomorrow when you pop round…if you pop round, that is…"

"Steady the Buffs!"

"…there's a power point in the garage for your drill. I'll leave the door open."

"Work, work, work," moaned Harper, as they were crossing the road.

"Talking of which, what are you working on at the Bank, anyway?"

"Drinks machine is on the blink. Can't do without their coffee, apparently."

"Didn't know you dabbled with that sort of thing."

"Not as a rule, no, but they're mostly electrics, when it all comes down to it, aren't they?"

Not having a clue about drinks machines and their internal workings, Crowther could only nod in agreement, but an idea had formed in his mind.

"Tell you what, Ian, will you do us a favour? Will you pop in the station tomorrow morning...say, about 8-ish? And bring your tools, eh?"

"If you like. What for?"

"There'll be folding money in it."

"Not yours, I bet. OK, I'll be there. Better press on."

Harper turned to go round the corner.

"Thought you were working here in the bank." said Crowther, pointing to the main entrance.

"I am, but I'm only a common or garden worker. I have to use the Tradesmen's Entrance. See you later."

Harper turned left and disappeared, as Crowther went up the steps to the main entrance of the Bank. As he reached the door, it opened, he stepped aside and out came Allyson, her friend Donna and another colleague from the bank, all chatting away. They walked straight past him and down the steps without even a glance. He fell in behind them as they continued their conversation along the High Street.

"Mrs. Allyson Crowther?" he asked, in a deep official-type voice.

The women turned, and Allyson said, "Yes…oh, good Lord, it's you, Colin. You nearly frightened me to death. What are you doing here?"

"I'm arresting you for having a fantastic bum."

"Colin!"

"Oh, yes, and what about us? Don't we qualify, as well?" Donna said, feigning offence.

"I'll let you off with a caution this time. Hello, Donna."

"Hello, Colin. Your husband's mad, Allyson, you do know that, don't you? See you later," she smiled and waved, as she and her colleague continued along the High Street.

"Bye," said Allyson and turned to Crowther. "So, to what do I owe this visitation?"

"No particular reason. I was just waiting for a couple of people to arrive, so I thought I'd go out on the pull. Fancy the Roebuck for a spot of lunch?"

"Suits me. They're off to McDonald's. I was dreading it, quite frankly. I can never get a Big Mac in my mouth all at once."

"There's no answer to that."

After they had crossed the High Street and were strolling towards the pub, Crowther said, "Actually, there was something I wanted to talk to you ab..."

"Oh, look at that! Oh, it's gorgeous, isn't it?"

Allyson had stopped outside Mothercare and was staring at a Silver Cross pram that was the centre-piece of its window display.

"Lovely," Crowther agreed, albeit rather unconvincingly.

"Shall we go in? Pretend? Oh, let's."

"Bad luck, they say. Anyway, times getting on," he said, looking at his watch and moving off.

"I suppose so. Another day, then, eh?"

Allyson looked longingly back at the window, as she caught up with him.

"So, what did you want to talk to me about?"

"It's nothing that can't wait. Let's have lunch."

"Come on, what is…"

Crowther's mobile rang and got him out of the hole he had just started digging for himself. "Crowther…yes, Parker, what is it?…good, tell him I'll be right there." He looked sadly at Allyson, kissed her on the cheek and apologized, "Sorry. Got to go. See you at home later."

Allyson watched him disappear towards Pemborough Police HQ. She smiled regretfully, turned away from the pub and resigned herself to the rigors of an imminent Big Mac.

*

Not more than half an hour later, in his office, Crowther was huddled with the sound engineer, as they listened to the playback of Sir Harold's answering machine. They were both on headphones and were listening to each part of John Goodland's messages again and again. There was a particular short section in one of them that Crowther was interested in but couldn't quite catch what was being said.

"You mean that bit?" said the engineer, pausing the replay.

"No, not that. I mean just after Goodland says 'Hi, it's John'."

The engineer found the message and replayed it.

"Seems quite clear to me. He says, 'Sorry about the noise. We're just leaving Oxford.' Can you not hear it?"

"Oh, I can hear that, yes, clear as a bell. What I'd like to be able to make out, though, is 'the noise' that he's talking about. Sounds like an announcement of some kind. Can you bring up that background level, so I can hear what it is?"

"Sure. Hang on a minute. I'll bring it up on my cans and try to fade out his voice."

The engineer's face was a study in concentration, as he strained to decipher what was going on in the background. Eventually, after listening for several minutes, he wrote something on a notepad and passed it to Crowther, who smiled as he read it.

"Terrific. Things might be starting to make sense. Thank you very much."

He pocketed the note, left his office and came face to face with DC Collins.

"The owner of the bike's just arrived, sir. He's not too happy about being dragged all the way up here, though."

"He'll grow out of it. Where is he?"

"Outside the front entrance. I told him he could park round the back and have a seat inside, but he seems reluctant to let the bike out of his sight."

*

The owner, sitting astride his sparklingly clean motorbike and dressed in full black leathers, was nursing a matching crash helmet, as if it were a babe in arms. He had a shaved head, sported a bushy moustache and looked every inch the tough biker. To those who didn't know any better, he would probably have looked a bit scary. To those who did know better, he was a pussycat and was on the butch side of the Brighton gay scene. Why Brighton was developing a reputation as the gay capital of the South probably had more to do with its immigrant gay and lesbian population than it had to do with any inherent desire of indigenous Brightonians to shake off the shackles of heterosexuality and 'come out' en masse, but then again, you never know.

"This is Detective Chief Inspector Crowther. This is Mr. Ellis, sir," said Collins.

"Afternoon, Mr. Ellis."

"Afternoon."

"There was no need to have brought the bike. We could have arranged transport."

"And risk having her nicked again? No way, babes. I keep her in the hall now, and I'm getting the bus to the station in future."

"Yes, I understand," said Crowther with a quick glance to Collins. "It must have been very distressing; being parted."

"Too right. You can pay for the petrol, though. It's a 250 mile round trip up to this neck of the woods, you know."

"Don't worry, Mr. Ellis, DC Collins will sort that out later. The point is, how much does your bike do to the gallon?"

"Depends, babes, doesn't it?"

"I'm sure it does…Mr Ellis, but when you came to collect it on erm…"

"Tuesday, it was. That was another day off work, I'll have you know."

"Tuesday, yes, of course. Now, I understand that at that time the tank was nearly full."

"Yes, well, I'll give you that, fair enough, but I still had to get back to Brighton, right? That's a big hole in it, you know, and I'm still entitled to the money for today."

"No problem. Anyway, forget the money, that's not the issue."

"As long as you don't, darling."

"I'm sure you'll remind us. However, the point at issue is this: how far do you reckon your bike had been driven since it was filled up, assuming it was filled up to the top, that is?"

"Why do you want to know that, for Christ's sake?"

"Could you just answer the question, please, Mr. Ellis? How far would your bike have travelled from where it had been filled up to where we found it?"

"You mean, up to when I came to collect it on Tuesday?"

"You got it. The tank was nearly full, wasn't it?"

"Yes, not too far off."

"So, from being full, how far, in miles would the amount of fuel used have taken the bike?"

"Depends, doesn't it? On how it was driven. Fast, slow, stop and start. Depends."

"Let's say, fast and pretty much non-stop."

"Well, let's see. You say it had been filled right up?"

"Let's assume that, yes."

"In that case, I'd say, 50 miles, give or take. 55 tops."

"Thank you. So, to be clear, from where we found this bike, and working backwards, it would be no more than 55 miles to where it was filled up? Are you sure about that?"

"I know my bike, babes. If I say 55 tops, it's 55 tops."

"Very well - 55 tops it is, then. Would you mind signing a statement confirming that?"

"Jesus Christ, she wants writing now!"

"It'll give my Detective Constable here time to sort out your money. Thank you very much, Mr.

Ellis. You've been extremely helpful. Excuse me." Crowther nodded and smiled to Collins and went up the steps to the main entrance.

"Is that it? I haven't even had a cup of tea."

"In this place? You'll be lucky, bab...Mr Ellis," Crowther threw the remark over his shoulder and disappeared.

"I'll bring you a cuppa out, shall I?" said Collins.

"Thanks, babes. Can't beat a nice cup of tea, can you. Have you got Earl Grey, by any chance?"

"I'll have to get back to you on that one." Collins smiled her reply and turned to go back into the station. "Won't be long."

*

The M40 motorway extension from Oxford to Birmingham had been a nightmare for the Department of Transport (DoT) for most of its twenty or more years of planning and building. The delay had been due principally to objections by local residents and Friends of the Earth over the planned crossing of what became known as Alice's Field (a reference to Lewis Caroll's 'Through the Looking-Glass', which partly inspired by the chess-board-like landscape of the area of Otmoor). In the end, the objectors bought the controversial field themselves, sold it off as 3500 separate lots and encouraged each subsequent purchaser to resist attempts at compulsory purchase by a beleaguered DoT, which eventually backed down and moved the planned route east, thus avoiding the beautiful area of Otmoor.

When Transport Secretary, Malcolm Rifkind, finally declared it open on January 15th, 1991, the M40 might have been a relief for the DoT and a blessing for the villages of Oxfordshire, but it still held its reputation as something of a nightmare, although this time for any motorist needing a Service Station - there weren't any.

The result of this mysterious omission was that 'four-star' Parker, driven by PC Tate, was having to scour the country roads of east and south-east Oxfordshire looking for petrol stations where Mr Ellis's motorbike might possibly have been filled up. It was beginning to feel like a thankless task.

Parker emerged from the office of the fifth small garage of the day and opened the car's passenger door.

"No joy. Again," he said, as he slumped into his seat next to PC Tate. "There must be dozens of petrol stations round here."

"A few, son. See, this 'ere M40 only opened this year and so far there's no Service Stations on it, otherwise he would have used one of them, wouldn't he? Course he would. Stands to reason. So, where to now?"

"Your guess is as good as mine. Probably better."

"Probably. Well, we're eighteen miles from Oxford now. How far did DCI Crowther say we should go up to…thirty, was it?"

"Yes, more or less," replied Parker, consulting his notebook. "According to our Mr Ellis, the bike's owner, it would have done - hang on, I've got it written down somewhere - yes, here we are '55 tops he said' since it was filled up. Now, we know it did twenty-seven miles from Oxford to Banbury, via the murder scene, therefore, it must have had petrol within a thirty-mile radius of Oxford, almost certainly south/southeast as it was coming from Brighton. Right, let's go along as far as Junction 5, Stokenchurch, have a scout round there and call it a day. Agreed?"

"Okey, dokey," said Tate, putting the car in gear and moving off. "As long as I'm home in time for the latest episode of The Bill, I don't care."

*

Later that evening, in Crowther's house, the music and the 'plodding feet' opening to that very episode of The Bill was on the TV, as Crowther relaxed by the open patio doors and scanned the local paper.

Allyson emerged from the kitchen carrying two plates of food.

"Dinner is served," she announced, delicately placing the plates on the dining table and fetching a bottle of their habitual Liebfraumilch from the sideboard.

Just as The Bill's DCI Burnside was making his entrance into the Sun Hill station, DCI Crowther silenced the TV with the remote and sat at the table.

"Wow! This looks nice. What is it?" he said, admiring the plateful of food.

"Coq au Transit," came the reply.

"Right," he smiled and started to open the bottle of wine.

"I saw Ian today. He was working at our branch," said Allyson.

"Yes, I know. I was chatting to him just before lunchtime. He was moaning about how him and Mary never used to get any sleep, or even go out, when they first had their kids."

"They don't know how lucky they were."

"No, I mean, yes…that's what I said," he replied tentatively, as he poured them each a glass of wine.

"Cheers!" He raised his glass and the phone rang. "Bugger. Do you know, I'll swear they have someone watching this house, just waiting until I sit down to eat."

He went to the sideboard and picked up the landline phone.

"Crowther…good, they there now?...what about the phone company?...right…yes, I'm on my way." He put the phone down and turned to Allyson. "Sorry, gotta go."

"We'll never have any kids at this rate, Colin."

"I thought this was Coq au Transit, not Coq au…"

"It's not a joke, Colin."

"No, sorry. Anyway, I thought the right time was last Sunday."

"It was, but the odd practice run wouldn't go amiss."

"Well, you said it would be better if I saved it all up."

"Did I? Well, I'd like to make a withdrawal, if it's all the same to you. You must have a scrotumful by now."

"I'm not a fucking machine, Allyson!"

"Ain't that a fact? And don't be crude!" she said and stared at him in disbelief, as he plowed on.

"Have you ever stopped to think what it's like for me, eh? No, I bet you haven't. I've got a job I've no control over; I have to rush out; I'm back at all hours and if I walk through that door without an erection, I've had my chips!"

"Don't be so melodramatic."

'Oh, 'melodramatic' am I? Well, I'm sorry, but it's true and it's getting me down. I wouldn't mind but we did it on Monday. It's only Thursday now!"

"So, when can I expect the next 'visitation'?"

"For God's sake! I don't know. Tomorrow. Take it or leave it."

"How could a girl resist such a charming invitation?"

"Well, it's the best I can do. For the love of God, don't keep on about it, will you? I've got to go. I'll see you later."

"You might."

"And what's that supposed to mea...oh, forget it. I'll...I'll be back."

Crowther grabbed his coat and stormed out, leaving Allyson close to tears.

*

It is never a good idea to drive under the influence of alcohol. It is an even worse idea to drive under the influence of a row with your wife.

The difference is that in the former case, which should never be attempted, of course, you'll at least be sober in the morning and, barring accidents, will have 'got away with it.' In the latter case, though, you'll wake up with the mother of all emotional hangovers (and with the mother of your children, too, if you're lucky), without a cat in hell's chance of getting away with anything else for at least a further twenty-four hours.

Many a man has been through it (never his fault, of course), and a sober Crowther was no exception as he tackled the narrow country lanes of south-east Oxfordshire. He obviously thought he was secure, cocooned in his car, and was ill-advisedly pushing up its speed in inverse proportion to the descent of dusk. However, his concentration was elsewhere and that feeling of security was about to have a rude awakening. He was in the middle of imagining Allyson reeling from his next killer speech (a subtle mixture of Churchill's wit and Henry Vth's inspiration), when he realized he was fast approaching a T-junction with the main through road from Oxford to Stokenchurch. Without even signaling, he braked and was swinging left when an almighty blast on a car horn brought him back to reality. Unlike Crowther, the driver of the car that had just swerved to avoid him had his concentration firmly fixed on the road ahead, instead of daydreaming about scoring debating points off his wife.

Crowther parked in the next gateway he could find, shook his head vigorously to regain concentration and decided that he just had to put the evening's spat with Allyson behind him. He made a pathetically biased and wholly unsatisfactory stab at persuading himself that he was in the right and she was in the wrong. Regardless, that had to suffice for the moment. That done, he carefully pulled out onto the road.

No more than half a mile further on, the flashing lights of a patrol car came into view. There were several Uniforms around, keeping whatever traffic there was on the move, and Forensic personnel were wandering in and out of the office premises of a small one-man-band garage. Above the door was a fading sign that read:

MAURICE WELLINGS GARAGE LIMITED

Crowther pulled up and got out of his car, to be met by a proud-looking PC Parker.

"It's a result, sir."

"Show me."

"Forensics are smiling as well," said Parker, as he handed over his notebook.

"That's a first," muttered Crowther, scanning the notebook. "Brilliant. Get Goodland in, but for God's sake don't let 'Absolutely' get wind of it."

"Who, sir?"

"Sorry, Parker. I forgot you're comparatively new to the job, aren't you? I mean, Chief Superintendent Vance, and let's just keep all this to ourselves for the moment, eh? Anyway, he'll never find a dry-cleaners open at this time of night."

"No, sir. Probably not," said Parker, blissfully unaware of what Crowther was talking about. "I'll get Goodland, sir."

"Yes. No! No, leave it. Half-eight in the morning will do. He's not going anywhere. Let's tie everything up here and call it a day. After all, everybody could do with an early night...I certainly could."

*

The sun had finally set on suburban Pemborough, leaving the Crowthers' back garden shrouded in darkness. Through the open patio doors, the sound of Meat Loaf's 'Bat out of Hell' drifted, or rather careered, out into the night, as Allyson lay on the sofa, enjoying the moment.

Meat, or Mr Loaf, whichever form of address you prefer, was just reaching one of his trademark climaxes, when the beam of a torch crossed the lawn and moved onto the patio.

Allyson was unaware of the footsteps crossing towards the open doors, until she heard a voice say, "Hello, darling." She spun round to see a face illuminated from below by the torch. She managed to stifle a scream as the voice said, "It's only me."

"You bastard!" she said, albeit tinged with a huge sigh of relief, as she recognized Crowther, silhouetted in the patio doors.

"You want to get your fence repaired you know. Any old nutter could just walk in...don't say it!"

Crowther entered and turned off the music.

"What on Earth was that you were listening to?"

"'Bat out of Hell', if you must know. Meat Loaf."

"Meat Loaf? What kind of a name is that? Started his career calling himself Spam, I suppose."

"I take it things went well?" Allyson asked. Crowther smiled and nodded. "I thought as much. So, you decided you might as well top off the evening by coming home and scaring the shit out of your wife. Was that it?"

"More or less - you go it in one. Here, I brought you these."

He handed Allyson a small box of chocolates (milk and plain).

"Am I allowed to know why?"

"Of course you are. I got them because I...well, the truth is, because they were half price."

"You really are pushing it, Colin," said Allyson, suppressing a smile.

"Point taken. Look, I apologise for earlier on. I mean it."

"Earlier on? What happened 'earlier on'?"

"You never noticed, then? Me behaving like a complete pillock."

"No, not really. You seemed quite normal to me," she smiled. "I'm sorry too."

"Yes, well, don't let it happen again!"

They looked at each other for a few seconds before bursting into laughter.

"Come here," demanded Allyson, beckoning him to join her on the sofa. She wrapped her arms around him, and they kissed passionately. Things were getting heavier, as they began to explore each other. Allyson let her hand slide down his body and began gently massaging him.

"Mmmm. That's nice," murmured Crowther. "There's something I really must tell you."

"Oh, yes? And what's that? Tell me."

"I'm dying for a pee."

Allyson tried to smack him across the backside, as he made a run for the downstairs loo.

CHAPTER NINE

Friday, August 16th, 1991: 8.05am

Crowther came out of his office, accompanied by Ian Harper, who had his bag of tools slung over his shoulder. They both took a sip from their respective plastic cups, and smiled at each other as they approached DC Collins, DS Banks and Sgt Beech, who were congregated around the drinks machine.

"Thanks, Ian. That's great," said Crowther, tossing his now empty cup into the bin.

Harper did the same and replied, "No sweat. Any more problems, let me know."

"I certainly will. See you tomorrow at squash. My treat. It's the least I can do."

"Go on, then, I'll let you! Cheers."

Harper headed for the way out, as Crowther passed the puzzled-looking group. He slowed down to hear what they were saying.

"I don't understand it," muttered Sgt Beech.

"Neither do I," added Banks

Collins stared at the machine.

"It's weird," she said, pushing one of the buttons. "What's going on? Whatever you press, you get tea!"

Crowther, a self-satisfied smile plastered across his face, carried on back to his office.

*

In Sir Harold Moorhouses's study, John Goodland stood by the desk, looking through a file of bank statements. He was so engrossed in mentally totting up how much his late father-in-law had left in hard cash that he failed to register that somebody had wandered along the hallway and entered the room.

"Morning, sir."

A startled Goodland swung round.

"Who the hell are you? What are you doing here?"

"Thought the uniform might be a bit of a give-away, sir. PC Parker, Pemborough Police."

"Oh, yes?"

"Sorry to disturb you, sir, but the front door was open, and the bell doesn't work, apparently."

"Apparently. What do you want?"

"DCI Crowther would like a word. He's sent me to take you down to Police HQ."

"Why can't he come out here?"

"He's rather busy at the moment. There's a car outside, if you wouldn't mind, sir," said Parker, indicating towards the door.

"Very well, if you insist."

Goodland threw the bank statements onto the desk and walked slowly past Parker towards the door.

*

Police interview rooms are not particularly cheerful places, but then that is not what they are designed to be. If anything, they are designed to be conducive to concentration, undisturbed by unnecessary decoration, furniture and, as far as possible, extraneous noise. Such was the room in which John Goodland found himself that Friday morning waiting for Crowther to make an appearance. Apart from a table, four chairs and a Car magazine that he had brought with him, his only company was a uniformed PC standing by the door. After being kept waiting for over half an hour and having finished an in-depth article on the advances in Formula 1 racing car design, he looked at his watch and smiled condescendingly at the PC. Goodland guessed, quite rightly, that any attempt at conversation would be fruitless, so went back to his magazine.

At that moment, Crowther and DC Collins entered and sat in the chairs opposite to him. As Collins placed a portable tape machine, which she had brought in with her, on the table, Crowther put down two bottles of water along with several plastic beakers and settled himself in his chair.

"Good morning, Mr Goodland," he said cheerily, pouring each of them some water.

"About time, I must say," complained Goodland, closing his magazine and leaning back in his chair.

"Sorry to keep you waiting."

"I should think so, too. What's this all about, anyway?"

Collins slotted a new tape into the official tape machine, which was fixed to the wall, turned it on and announced, "Interview with John Goodland. Friday, 16th August, 9.15am..."

"Look, whatever you want to know, make it quick, will you? I've got to be out of here by ten o'clock, otherwise I'll be late for a test drive at Silverstone."

"...present: DCI Crowther, DC Collins.'

"Well, go on then. Don't tell me you've actually established my father-in-law's killer at last."

"As a matter of fact, we believe we have."

"You surprise me," unfazed, Goodland took a sip of water. "Have you arrested him?"

"Not yet, I'm afraid…"

"Typical!"

"…but I'm just about to. John Goodland, I am arresting you for the murder of Sir Harold Moorhouse. You do not have to say anything, unless you wish to do so, but anything you do say may be given in evidence."

"Oh, very good. Very good. You know, I didn't realise this was a stand-up comedy venue. Come off it. You've already got Graham Kirk for that, I understand."

"Mr Kirk is under arrest, as a matter of fact, but for an unrelated matter. Now, let me take that supercilious smile off your face, shall I?"

Collins gave Crowther a cautioning look, which he ignored. He was determined to enjoy himself, reeling Goodland in.

"Do you often use the telephone, Mr Goodland?"

"What? Oh, quite often, yes. What's that got to do…"

"Thought so. There's a nice, natural manner about your voice. Let's listen, shall we, while I play a recording from the answering machine in Sir Harold Moorhouse's study? Thank you, Collins."

She pressed 'play' on the portable recorder, and Goodland's voice could be heard.

'Hi, it's John. Sorry about the noise. (a whistle has blown, and an on-train announcement has begun in the background) *We're just leaving Oxford on the train. I'll try you in half an hour. Cheers.'*

Collins stops the tape.

"Was a bit noisy, wasn't it?" ventured Crowther.

"It certainly was." Goodland replied, taking more water, as his way of gaining thinking time to work out what Crowther was up to. "But then, that's trains for you."

"How true. Interestingly, our sound engineer managed to isolate the on-train Guard's announcement that was in the background. He was saying: *'...calling at Birmingham International, Birmingham New Street etc...'* Took the engineer quite a while, of course, but he does have the most up-to-date equipment."

"Really. Amazing thing - technology - don't you think?"

"Where would we be without it? Funny thing is, if that train was leaving Oxford, the Guard would have been saying, '...*calling at Banbury, Birmingham International, Birmingham New Street etc...* '"

"So?"

"So...you left that misleading message as the train was leaving Banbury, didn't you? You said you were leaving Oxford, so there would be recorded evidence (on the answering machine that you deliberately switched on after you murdered Sir Harold); evidence that, if needed, would prove you were on the train between Oxford and Banbury. But...you weren't on the train between Oxford and Banbury, were you, Mr Goodland? Because you got off the train at Oxford."

"Huh! Why on earth would I do all that? You're making it up," protested Goodland and took a long swig of water. "In any case, the Guard probably said...'*next stop Banbury, then...calling at Birmingham International and wherever...*' and that's the bit your brilliant sound engineer managed to isolate, as you put it. Highly likely that's what happened. Did you ask the Guard?"

"Yes, we did. He can't remember exactly what he said that day."

"Oh, dear. What a shame. Bang goes your theory, eh?"

"Not entirely. You see, there was another message on Sir Harold's answering machine."

"Yes, I phoned back later. We were just coming into Banbury."

"Were you really? But, no, not that one…this."

Crowther nodded to Collins, who pressed 'play' again. After a short pause and a beep, a woman's voice came out loud and clear:

'Harold, its Edith. I'll pop round in a while with those plants, if that's all right. If not, ring me. Bye.'

Collins paused the machine. Crowther didn't say a word, but with the faintest of smiles playing on the corners of his mouth, he looked straight at Goodland.

"What's that got to do with me?" a mystified Goodland, asked.

"Nothing at all, in a sense…except we know, from Mrs Edith Rowntree herself and from her phone records, that she called and left that message at 5.11pm. We also know, from Sir Harold's answering machine, that her message preceded yours. So, you must have called after 5.11pm. Now, since we also know that your train was on time and left Oxford at 4.59pm, you couldn't possibly have been making that call as the train was leaving Oxford, like you said you were, because the train had already left twelve minutes previously. You must have made that call as the train was leaving Banbury."

"Oh, is that what you're on about? Well, maybe it was...I don't know...Banbury. Stations are much the same, you know. Anyway, even if I did make the call when the train was leaving Banbury, what does it prove?"

"It proves that you weren't 'nearing Banbury' as you said you were in your second call, and therefore your alibi of being on the train between Oxford and Banbury has bitten the dust. Even your wife says she didn't see you then."

"Why on earth would I need an alibi?"

"Because you bashed your father-in-law's brains in, that's why!"

"No, Constable, it won't do. Supposing I did make those calls after Banbury, how does that prove I got off the train? Think about it."

"Were you born an arrogant bastard, or did it come by degrees?"

"For the tape, Constable Crowther is losing it," said a smug Goodland.

"Listen, clever bollocks, I hate talking to you as much as you hate talking to me, but, by God, you're going down for this."

Goodland had made a really good job of winding Crowther up, to such an extent that Collins felt she had to step in and defuse a situation that was on the verge of becoming violent. She put a calming hand on Crowther's arm and spoke quite softly to Goodland.

She said, "Mrs Ivy Wellings has recovered from her hip replacement operation, you'll be glad to know."

"What's this woman rattling on about now?'

"Oh, of course, you haven't had the pleasure of meeting dear old Ivy, have you? Lovely lady, they say, don't they, sir?"

"Yes, indeed, that's what they say," Crowther smiled at Collins and winked. "Carry on, Collins, please."

"Thank you, sir. You've met her husband, of course."

"Her husband? I haven't the foggiest idea what you're talking about."

"I'm sure you must remember Maurice Wellings, Mr Goodland."

"Who?"

For the first time, Goodland's mask of total confidence showed signs of slipping.

"What's she wittering about?"

Crowther, having calmed down, took over from Collins, and said, "I'll tell you what she's wittering about, shall I, although it's a story you know well. After all, you are the hero of it."

"Oh, get on with it, for God's sake,' Goodland was looking at his watch. "It's getting on for ten o'clock. I haven't much time left you know."

"How true. How very true. I've got a story to tell you. Let me start at the beginning:

You left home at 6.30am last Thursday morning. You went to your office, where you picked up the black crash helmet and the pair of metal cutters you'd bought, and a sheet of Technical Drawings that Graham Kirk had been handling the day before, when he was there (your little 'fingerprint frame-up'). You put the lot in your hold-all and left."

"As you said, it's a story. Read a lot of fiction, do you?"

"Bear with me, sir. You walked to Brighton Railway Station and waited for a particular motorbike to arrive. You knew it would turn up, because you had been there every day for I-don't-know-how-long watching. You waited until the owner's train had left, freed the bike's chain with the cutters, which you put in the hold-all for use later to kill Sir Harold. You

237

knew the owner kept a spare set of keys in the wing mirror. You'd seen them used."

"Where on earth did you get all that nonsense from?" said Goodland, laughing.

"A lot of it is speculation, I grant you. However, you drove that Suzuki bike out of Brighton...up the M23...round the M25...and onto the M40...by that time, it was past 9.15am and you realized that you desperately needed petrol. Service Stations haven't yet been built on the M40, so you went off at Junction 5, found a small one-man-band garage, belonging to a certain Maurice Wellings, and filled up the bike."

"I see. Yet more speculation. I'm waiting for some sort of proof to emerge from your charming story. So far, nothing."

"Patience. Patience. You then carried on to Oxford Railway Station car park, and at 10.07am bought an all-day parking ticket, stuck it on the bike and went to the ticket office. There, you bought a return ticket to Brighton and a single from Banbury to Birmingham International. You boarded the 10.22am to Brighton, arriving shortly after 1.00pm. You got to your office shortly before 1.30pm, phoned for a taxi, picked up your wife and got to Brighton Railway Station well in time to catch the 2.15pm train to Manchester."

"That last part of your story is correct, I agree, although it's the only part that is. Please carry on, Constable, I'm intrigued."

"Just before the Manchester train reached Oxford, your wife told us that you said you were going to get her something to eat, and you borrowed her phone to call Sir Harold about some technical problems with the F1 car's gear box."

"Correct again. You are doing well."

"However, when the train stopped at Oxford, you got off, used the return half of the ticket you'd bought earlier and passed through the barrier. You retrieved the bike from the car park and drove to Sir Harold's house. When you got there, you used the cutters from your hold-all to kill him. You left the technical papers, containing Graham Kirk's fingerprints, on the desk, turned on the answering machine and left.

You drove at speed to Banbury Railway Station, left the bike in the car park and used the single ticket from Banbury, which you'd bought in Oxford earlier, to pass quickly through the barrier. You were on the platform in time to get back on the same train that you had left at Oxford, and, as the train was leaving, you made the two calls to Sir Harold's answering machine. In the first of those calls you said you were 'leaving Oxford' and would call back in half an hour. In the second call you said you were 'nearing Banbury'. You then went to rejoin your wife. All of which, as far as the recordings on the answering machine were concerned, established beyond doubt that you had been on the train the whole time, and created what you thought was the perfect alibi."

"And so it is. It's perfect. Not that I need an alibi, of course. I've nothing to hide. Well, it's a very good story indeed, I grant you. The trouble is, by your own admission, it is speculation. Apart from what my wife told you, which is absolutely correct, there isn't a scrap of truth in the whole thing, leave alone the slightest shred of evidence or proof."

"Oh, I don't know. I thought we'd done rather well on that score."

"In what way exactly?"

"Since you ask, let me take you back to the ubiquitous Maurice Wellings and his wife's hip replacement operation."

"If you must. Who the hell is he anyway?"

"Maurice? He's the owner of the garage where you stopped to fill up the bike."

"Where you say I stopped. I've never been there. I don't even know where it is."

"Oh, yes, you do, and you were there last Thursday morning at around 9.30am."

"Really?"

"Yes, really. You see, it was just after 9.25am when you pulled onto Maurice's garage forecourt and, although you didn't know it, he was about to close up for a fortnight and take his wife, Ivy, into hospital for her hip replacement operation.

You told him to fill up the bike, while you went to use his pay phone. According to Maurice, your actual words were: 'Fill her up.' You then snapped your fingers and demanded, 'Phone! Where is it?' Maurice ignored your rudeness and pointed along the passage towards the toilets: the pay phone was on the left, perhaps you remember. The call you made was to your wife in Brighton. She has told us that in the call she received from you at about 9.30am that morning, you said, 'I'm at the office. I'll order a cab about half past one and pick you up. I'll be in the Design Office all morning, so you won't be able to ring me.' You paid for the petrol in cash and left."

"How the hell was I supposed to do all that when I was in Brighton, for God's sake? You're going to tell me next that he recognized me, I suppose."

"No, he couldn't do that. You kept the helmet on all the time you were in his sight. A deliberate ploy to stop him seeing your face."

"Oh, for crying out loud. It's all fantasy. It's based on nothing,"

"Not entirely. Maurice locked up and went home. When we tracked him down and got him to open up his garage, nothing had been touched. Everything was exactly as it was when he had locked up...including the phone. Pressing 'recall', we found that the last call, which, according to Maurice had been made by 'the rude motorcyclist who stopped for petrol last Thursday', was to your home number. That was confirmed when we heard this:

'You've reached John and Anna Goodland. You know the routine. Leave a message and we'll get back to you. Thanks for calling. Bye.'

Quite a coincidence, eh? Your wife getting a call at 9.30am, and that last call from the garage being made to your number, also at 9.30am."

Goodland's face told that he was feeling the heat of Crowther's revelations. Nevertheless, he tried desperately to salvage anything he could.

"If you're implying that I made that call, you're sadly mistaken. You know damn well it could have been anybody."

"Not just anybody. Don't forget, we know that that call was made by a motorcyclist who stopped for petrol at about 9.30am last Thursday morning. Why would some anonymous motorcyclist, riding through deepest Buckinghamshire, suddenly decide to phone you at home in Brighton? Unless, of course, you're on intimate terms with the Buckinghamshire motorcycling fraternity. Do you have a particular friend among them?"

"Yet more speculative rubbish. It was just a…wrong number. Anyway, I keep telling you, I was in Brighton."

"No, you weren't. We also found two sets of fingerprints on the phone. One belonged to Maurice Wellings; the other matched a set of prints given to us for elimination purposes at Sir Harold's house…by you."

"You can't have got my prints. For a start, I was…well, you can't have."

"Wearing gloves? Is that what you were going to say? Were you, indeed? Thank you for that, Mr. Goodland. Now I come to think of it, yes, of course you would have been. However, you must have taken them off, mustn't you? How else could you have 'snapped your fingers' at Maurice? And you kept them off so you could use the phone, didn't you?

Interestingly, those prints we managed to lift, and the prints at Sir Harold's, also matched the ones on the cutters that you threw out of the train and which were found in a field bordering the railway line just outside Banbury. Those cutters were covered in Sir Harold's blood. The proof of the pudding…as they say.

For the tape, Mr. Goodland has wiped the smile off his face. Interview terminated 9.22am."

EPILOGUE

Dining 'al fresco' needs a certain climate to make it truly part of any country's culinary culture. Thus, the English, being somewhat meteorologically challenged, tend not to indulge too often in the joys of outdoor eating. However, special occasions call for special measures. Such a special occasion was Allyson's birthday on that Friday, which called for the special measure of the Crowthers eating out on the patio.

Their starters, comprising prawn cocktails in a Marie Rose sauce, along with an open bottle of their habitual Liebfraumilch, were laid out on the garden table. Crowther was inside by the patio doors fixing a plug, while Allyson was opening her presents. She had already been delighted with the pair of black trousers from Marks (size 10, £35), a bottle of Sainsbury's in-house champagne (non-vintage) and a bouquet of flowers from the garage down the road (price-tag still attached). She was absolutely stunned when she opened the Shalimar perfume and discovered that it wasn't what she assumed it must be, Eau de Toilette, but was, in fact, the real thing.

"Oh, Colin, you shouldn't have," she cooed, being ever so glad that he had.

"I know I shouldn't, but I did."

"Thank you. It's just what I wanted, and it's the real thing."

"Don't I know it. Not bad for a wild guess, was it? Here's something else you wanted, but thought you'd never get. Wait for it. Here we go."

Crowther pressed the plug switch and the Garden Lights came on, looking quite stunning in the gathering dusk.

"Oh, Colin, not Garden Lights as well. They look really, really nice. I told you they would. I'm being spoilt. Thank you so much."

"My pleasure," said Crowther, pouring the wine and handing a glass to Allyson. "Have a drink."

"Thank you."

"Happy Birthday…oh, I nearly forgot. Here."

He had produced a small package from his pocket and handed it to her.

"Not more?" she could hardly believe it. She opened the package to reveal a pair of thong-type knickers. "And just what is the idea of these?"

"To keep you warm, what else?"

As Allyson held them up, a piece of paper dropped out.

"And what's this? The bill, I suppose, knowing you."

"Well that's where you're wrong, madam. It's a poem…for you."

"Awww. You really love me, don't you? Read it for me. Go on, please."

"Ok, if you insist:

There's one small gift that's missing here,
It's a daughter or a son.
So, when you've done the washing-up,
I thought I'd give you one.

How about that?"

Allyson didn't know whether to laugh or cry. She did both.

"That is so, so lovely. You have no idea. Well, you're on. Here's to the three of us." She raised her glass.

Crowther watched her take a drink.

"Yes. To the three of us," he smiled weakly and downed his drink in one. As he did so, the Garden Lights went out with a pop. "Oh, shit!"